Destiny Stained

Shradha Agarwal

Inkfeathers Publishing

Destiny Stained
Written by Shradha Agarwal

First Published in India in 2021
Inkfeathers Publishing
New Delhi 110095

ISBN - 9789390882496

www.inkfeathers.com

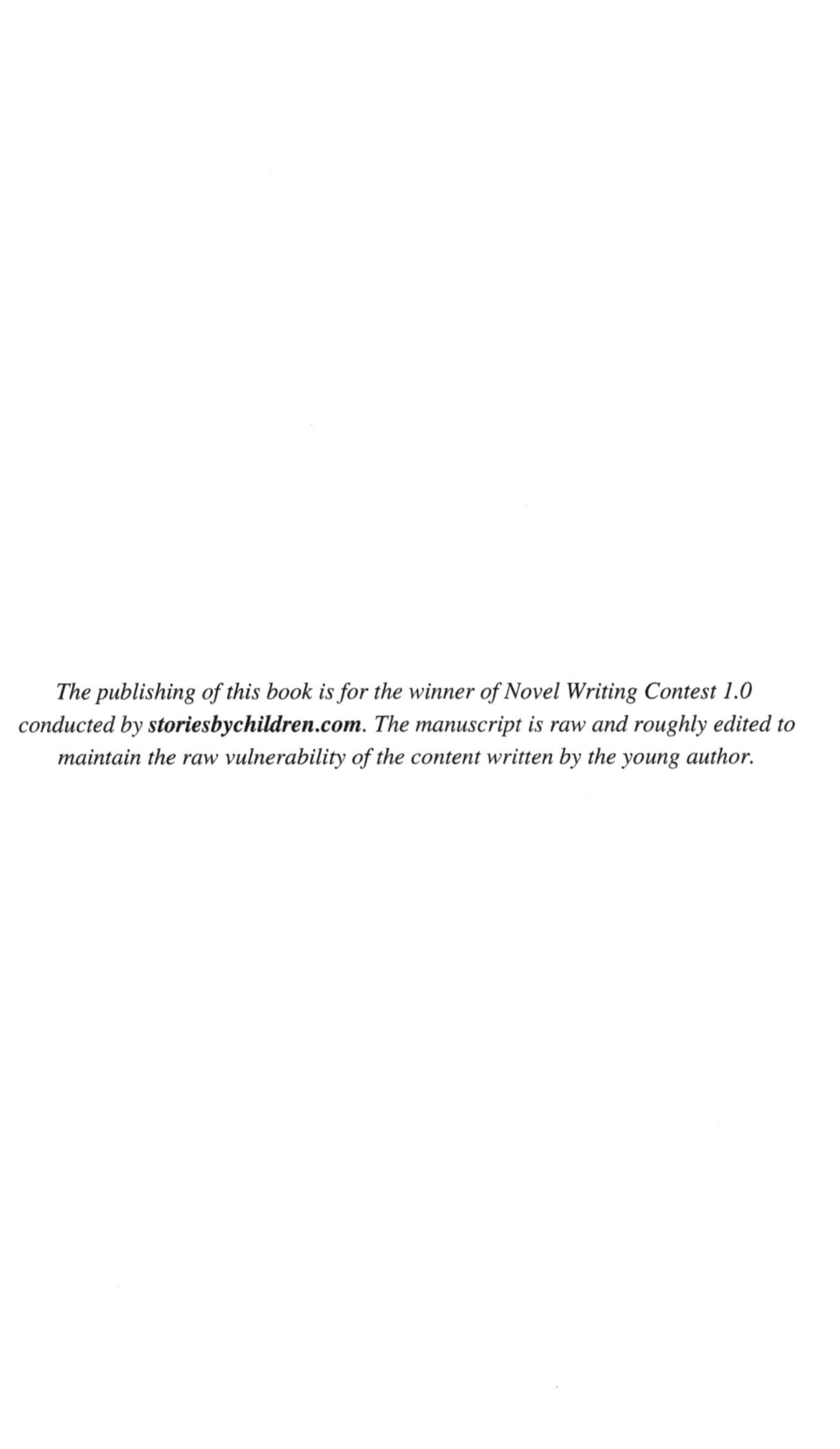

Contents

About the Author

Acknowledgements

About the Judge

Our Sponsors

Other Activities

About Stories By Children

Kids, teens, adults - everyone loves stories. For ages, we have heard stories from Grandma, Grandpa, Mama, Papa, Teachers, and others narrate stories that inspire us, teach us, enlighten us and entertain us. We have heard stories from various authors.

Now, it's time for the kids to show their talent. Kids have amazing levels of creativity and imagination and this is what can birth stories that will blow our minds. We at Stories By Children let their thoughts flow and wander to bring their imagination to life in the form of stories, articles, or poetry. We encourage them to think out of the box and guide them to access their ability to pen down their creativity.

We as a writing community are here to encourage those budding writers and give them a platform to showcase their literary skills. We also encourage those young readers too, who by reading the stories and poems can inspire others and themselves to write more and read more and expand their minds to unimaginable horizons.

This is a safe space for young writers to express themselves - a place for them to share their thoughts and let the world know how you are different.

Stories By Children is a non-profit organization that allows for a free platform for young writers, readers, and poets to participate in various activities for absolutely free. There is no registration fee to join us. Simply visit our website **www.storiesbychildren.com** and register yourself and start submitting your work.

Stories By Children is a strong team of 16 people with reviewers, editors, social media managers, graphic designers, and a web development team. You could also join us and volunteer your time to help us keep this platform safe and free for all writers and readers.

Join us today as an intern, volunteer, contributor, sponsor, editor, or reviewer. You can write to us at **info@storiesbychildren.com** or call us **+91 86604 77790** or simply register yourself as a reviewer on our website **www.storiesbychildren.com/Home/ReviewerRegistration**

Stories By Children is growing and we'd love for you to grow with us. If you have a small business and would like to invest, donate or sponsor, please contact us using the details mentioned above. We are open to advertising and/or collaborating with you anytime.

Today, Stories By Children is home to over 700 stories by 300+ authors with about 1000+ readers and supporters. We can grow and expand our operations furthermore only with your love and support. Spread the word. Invite readers and young writers to join us and grow. Readers of any age group are welcome to register on the website and start reading and supporting the work submitted by these young budding writers.

Like our Facebook Page **@Stories By Children**

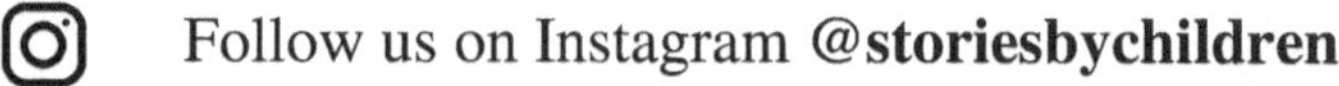
Follow us on Instagram **@storiesbychildren**

Tweet about us and tag us **@the_sbc_tweets**

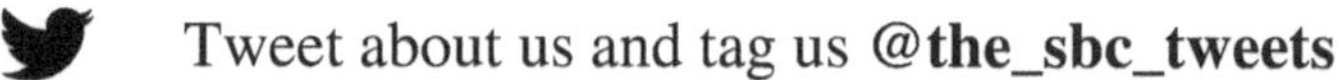
Find us on LinkedIn **@storiesbychildren**

Reviews

This book is a treat to all the mystery lovers and is bound to leave you amazed. The plot is beautifully woven with twists and turns to keep the reader glued to the book. Not revealing a clue of who the murderer is and what the story is all about till the end, it is going to be hard to keep the book aside.

Tanmayee Kalebar
Founder and Director of Stories By Children

The novel *Destiny Stained* written by Shradha Agarwal has a great plot. The characters are well etched out and the narration is fast-paced leading to intriguing suspense. Shradha has shown an incredible imagination and penchant for writing. Each book is a learning experience and Shradha has a bright future as an author.

Manoj Vaz
Author and Judge for 15-18 Category

This book is the paradigm of Shradha's imagination, creativty and talent. Right from the story plot to the way the charachters are woven, everything about the book is interesting. You may want to make yourself a cup of coffee before you begin because this book will keep you up reading all night.

Kashish Lewis
Editor and Graphic Designer at Stories By Children

Foreword

With the little conversations I had with Shradha over the phone, she seems to be an avid reader. That, as I get to know, is her inheritance from her father who has a library at home and is a reader himself. Her knowledge and imagination from reading are evident in her writing.

This book is a treat to all the mystery lovers and I am sure it will be their favourite. This novel from Shradha is bound to leave you amazed. How an uneventful, calm evening turns out to be the worst nightmare for Grace is surely going to keep you hooked till the end. The plot is beautifully woven with twists and turns to keep the reader glued to the book. Not revealing a clue of who the murderer is and what the story is all about till the end, it is going to be hard to keep the book aside.

The story lingers in the mind long after one has finished reading She was definitely a worthy choice to win this contest with her marvellous piece of work. Congratulations to Shradha and thanks to her well-wishers who have supported her dream of writing.

Wishing her the best on this new journey!

Mrs Tanmayee Kalebar
Founder and Director
storiesbychildren.com

Author's Note

Hello Reader!

Thank you for picking up this book and giving a new home to my work. I'm a 16-year aspiring sophomore. I started my journey of writing when I was 13 with short poems and stories. My hobbies include binging on Kdramas, listening to music, binging on Kpop Music, reading rom-com and fiction, journalising my thoughts and much more. More of a free soul, I like speaking on various issues and topics and also aspire to become a public speaker. I'm a total wanderlust! I believe travelling is one of the most essential spheres in my life.

I would like to thank **storiesbychildren.com** for giving young writers like me an opportunity and a platform to express and explore writing. I would further thank my parents, CA Sanjay Agarwal and Vandana Agarwal for their constant love and support towards my passion and my sister Astha who was always there to help me out with every dilemma I was in. I also thank my friends (VBRSV) who have been always encouraging me to go forward no matter what!

I hope you enjoy reading this much as I enjoyed writing it.

Shradha Agarwal
Author

Chapter 1
All About Grace

Grace looked outside the window. Small drops of rain were splashing on her window panel. It was raining all day and it was nearly evening. She sighed as she gazed outside the light fog. Winter was around the corner and the smell of rain created an aesthetic atmosphere. The light breezes hit her red cheeks and her numb eyes, tears wanted to escape but were bound by her determination of not letting them escape anymore.

Grace Thompson is a law graduate and had turned 24 this year. She was graceful, true to her name. Hardworking and diligent, she won many hearts and cases in her ex-firm. She was known for dedication and discipline at work. Probably this was the reason she never made a lot of friends at work. Sharp and hard-working, she solved all her cases with dedication. She was also awarded the best employee award twice in a row. Obviously, she became the talk of the firm and had more haters than followers.

There is a popular saying, Envy spreads much faster and lasts much longer than Love. The few friends that Grace had, changed with time and began to show their true colours. They started avoiding her and spread tons of fake news against her! They were simply jealous of her success and hated her gut. For a 23-year-old girl, who had just started living life, who finally thought that she could be independent, this was too much to handle.

Grace would often break down and suffer from anxiety. Being alone and being lonely has a huge difference. Loneliness hit Grace hard, she suffered from acute depression of being alone all the time. But, she never let it out to the world. She submerged all her pain and focused on her career, her only love in life. Probably, that was the reason for her to live life.

The chairman of the firm, Mr. Noh was a small, fat man who adorned himself with gold. He was a vinegar tempered person to whom success meant everything. Mr. Noh had an only child, Zain. He adored him more than anything and spoilt him to great extents. Being the only rich inheritor, Zain was rude to everyone. He was a famous idol, having a sharp and heart-throbbing appearance. His career was made out of his father's financial support. He was an extremely talented singer but his rudeness and his temper often made him hot searches. He had lakhs of fans and his voice sounded like sunshine on a rainy day. But his behaviour was always very annoying for Grace. She was the only person who actually spoke to Zain, but those weren't usually words but heated arguments.

Zain used to walk into the firm casually and insult any staff member passing by. He'd pass sarcastic comments or exchange a scornful look for a good morning. Success blinded him and his attitude pierced people.

Once, in an unlucky sphere, Zain threw a glass of water on an old staff, just because the water wasn't cold enough. Grace was so furious about it; they had a hot argument that day. They were screaming at the top of their voices. It was more like Grace was shouting at him, while Zain stood there cool, unresponsive with a face of no regret. That agitated her more. She hated when people looked down on staff or other workers. Zain and her fights were popular in the whole office. But there was something about Grace, her attitude, her coldness or her creativity, something always attracted Zain.

Grace blinked quickly trying to forget her dark past, she sipped the remaining coffee - it was calm and hot. She decided to go for another cup with some instant noodles. She walked to the fridge and found that there were none of the items she wanted. She grunted. It was cold and she didn't want to go outside.

She breathed heavily and walked towards her door. She picked up a few envelopes outside in her letterbox and as soon as her eyes skimmed through, her eyes were filled with worry. Her electricity and rent both were due. She threw away the envelopes in annoyance and walked to the flea market.

She recollected her past. All the moments flashed in front of her. Youth is mysterious and at the same time very dangerous. Zain was hit by the fire of youth and he succumbed to the burns.

Once, at a bar, he ordered a wine bottle but the waiter brought the wrong item. Zain smashed the bottle hard on the floor and openly abused the young boy. He wasn't the good kind of sober either. Now that he was drunk, his inner devil couldn't be controlled. His boiling blood wasn't pacified, he caught the boy by his collar and pushed him on the ground. The boy still appeared to be calm and didn't fight back, he was young but was not indecisive. He looked down and trembled and asked Zain to let it go. Arguments to fist-blows - the young lad was surrounded by Zain and his three friends and they smacked him mercilessly.

One of the friends hit the boy with a glass on the head. The huge smash was followed up by a terrifying silence. The bar was filled with people but no one stepped forward to help the young boy! Another huge chair smashed on the lad and he fell down with a thud. Drops of blood surrounded the floor, his white shirt soaked in blood! Luckily, the manager stepped in at that time and stopped Zain! Another young waiter jumped forward and called the ambulance. The boy ended up at a hospital lying in a coma. His upper head was damaged badly and he suffered many physical injuries.

Grace decided to solve the case at any cost. She worked very hard on the case. After checking the CCTV footage from the bar she was enraged. She looked at that teen, being assaulted by three grown-ups. She looked at the broken pieces of the bottle and the calm boy holding it in for so long.

She was adamant about having Zain punished.
Enough was enough!

Grace tried her best to fight back and explain to the chairman how important it is to teach Zain a lesson. Finally, irritated and furious with her activities, the chairman fired her. She became jobless and her talent fell gushing down just like the pouring rain. She came back to her senses. Ah, her wounds were still fresh

She walked downstairs. There was silence and only the sound of slow breezes were heard. Most of the people were off on a vacation. She moved down with her home slippers whistling to herself. She reached down and was walking to the nearby store. The roads were empty except for a few cars moving here and there. The rain had almost stopped but the little drops were still falling on the little puddles on the ground. The light breeze touched her faint cheeks. She didn't regret coming out for a walk, it was not only refreshing but also peaceful.

As she reached the local market, she laid her eyes on the coffee maker. It was huge, cool and at the same time very attractive. Grace touched the faint brown panels on the coffee machine. She wanted to buy it, but she clearly knew her financial conditions. She turned around and picked up a bottle of instant coffee and some instant noodles. She further walked the alleys and bought some vegetables.

She remembered her worn-out knife.

"Please give me the sharpest knife you have."

The shopkeeper handed her a stainless steel knife.

"This knife is enough to pierce through a person." He joked.

Grace laughed over the dead humour of the shopkeeper.

Her smile deepened, it was after a long time, she smiled.

She ruffled through a few more items as she heard a familiar voice. She turned back to see a tall man with broad shoulders. His brown hair flipped over his forehead, his eyes glistened in the fading light and his dimples engraved as he looked at Grace.

"Oh my my! Look who is here. Grace. It's been a long time."

The deep voice chuckled. There was calmness followed by a smirk as the deep blue eyes pierced Grace. Grace rolled her eyes as she noticed it was the person who brought hell to her - Zain. Avoiding him she continued,

"Sir, can you please bill these?"

The shopkeeper nodded as he continued fidgeting on his computer. The atmosphere was tense. Except for the sound of the keyboard, there was silence. The shopkeeper awkwardly handed the package to Grace.

Zain, instantly spoke, "Looks like you are still ignoring me. It has been nearly half a year. I will get my dad to bring you back - just kill your ego for a while, Okay? I really don't understand why

you are so hell-bent on destroying my career. It definitely isn't envy, so why this hatred towards me?"
He looked into her eyes and then turned his gaze away.
"I admit my fault, okay? But that does not give you the right to destroy The Zain Noh."
Grace picked up the knife in her hand as she said angrily,
"Another word and I will not spare you!"
The shopkeeper stepped backwards and said,
"Ma'am, careful. It is pretty sharp," he paused hesitantly.
"...and it isn't actually meant to pierce through someone."
Grace tossed it back in the shopping bag as she mumbled,
"The sharper the better." The shopkeeper stood perplexed.
"People like him need to be stabbed to death anyways."
The shopkeeper gulped while listening to the words of Grace.
Grace picked up her bag and walked outside as fast as possible.
Zain chuckled and followed her. He shouted,
"Come on. Stop ignoring me. I came to meet someone and found you. Luck is with me, maybe."
Grace didn't stop. She walked, her hair bouncing off with her. The sun had already set and the rain was getting heavier! Zain bubbled with anger when she just wouldn't listen but continued following her. Grace took bigger and more hurried steps as she saw him following her. Grace shuffled her brown hair backwards as she took huge leaps. She knew Zain, he was a good person, but something about the atmosphere and the tension between them gave her weird vibes. It was almost sunset. Home was still a few blocks away for Grace. The sun disappeared and the sky was dark now. The silence in the alleys was almost as if the world came to a standstill. Everything was dark, Grace started trembling. She hurriedly switched on her phone and then her flashlight.

A string of white light hit the front lane, there was no one. She realized that the footsteps of Zain were no longer heard. She felt a sting in her body. At the very next moment, she felt the presence of someone behind her a few meters away. She turned back pointing her flashlight in the nothingness. She could see a faint distant figure. It was Zain he stood there frozen. Grace knew there was something off about that vibes and that atmosphere. The rain hit her hair hard, her spectacles dripped in water. She gulped slightly and let out a small sigh.

She moved towards him and looked straight into the blue eyes of Zain. There was panic, pain, and anxiety as if his eyes silently called for help. Grace slowly moved closer.

There was a man standing right behind Zain. He was tall and muscular, he was wearing a mask. His face wasn't visible, but his scar shined in the flashlight. His black hair was drenched in rain and his eyes looked straight at her. His eyes were different. They showed too many emotions at once. Grace was scared but she could read his eyes. There was a strong emotion. Whether it was greed or sadness, she couldn't figure it out.

Her eyes moved to his stomach.

Oh my! Is that a knife?

Grace trembled as she focused on the knife.

It was deep red with drops of red blood dripping down. Her eyeballs adjusted to the darkness. She could now see clearly, Zain's white shirt was dished out in red. Grace looked at the man again, she opened her mouth to scream when the man instantly pushed Zain towards Grace.

Grace held him in her arms.

Her eyes widened, she looked back at Zain.

His eyes slowly closed. Grace's breath became erratic. She looked at the pierced red knife and pulled it out from his stomach. The man ran away in the opposite direction.

The shopkeeper stepped out of his shop to turn on his lights. His eyes focused on 2 people hugging each other in the distance. He walked closer. The expressions on Grace's face made him uneasy. As he reached them, he was shocked to see Zain in Grace's arms with drops of blood dripping on the ground and a knife in her hand with bloodstains. Grace stood without moving.

He covered his mouth and instantly called the police, trembling. Grace looked at Zain, who was in her arms lifeless. She dropped him in fear and shock. She looked at Zain collapse to the ground. She fell to her knees, she started shivering. she looked at her hands, they were covered in blood. She turned her gaze towards the lifeless Zain. She bit her lower lip and wrapped her cold hands around her. She couldn't move an inch. All she could see was the lifeless Zain covered in red; that was when she heard the sound of the police siren.

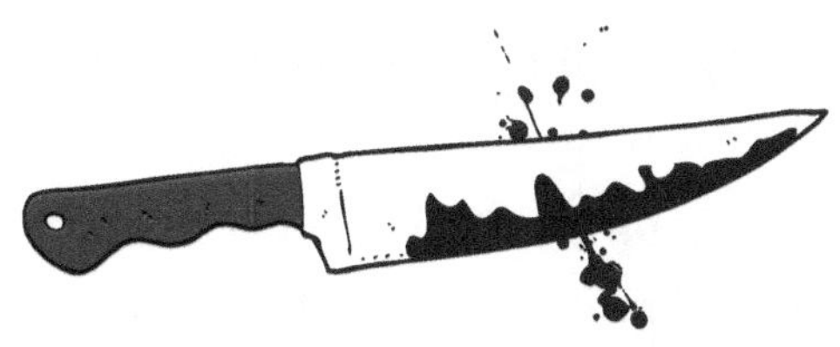

Grace wanted to stand up and explain what happened, but her legs were numb from shock and her lips were patched dry, her throat was filled with agony, fear and pain. She was too stunned to move.

The police arrived sooner than expected.

A muscular man stepped out of his car and looked at Zain on the ground lifeless and Grace trembling beside him. The man looked strict. He wore a polo neck shirt and his uniform was neatly ironed. His muscles were plopping underneath and his expressions were grim. He took the knife with the help of gloves and plopped it in a plastic bag. He whispered something and a female officer picked up Grace and pushed her inside the van.

Grace slowly sat down in the van, her eyes were still on the stain of blood on her palm. She reached the station and sat down in the chair shivering in shock with her hands and body soaked in blood. She was terrified by what had happened. The female police force tried questioning her but she sat there without moving.

The word of Zain being murdered spread like fire in a forest! The whole city nearly became aware of the murder in a few minutes. The online websites and news reporters hoarded the station and there were various articles published the very next minute. Grace was already labelled a criminal and the most looked down on the person in minutes.

Another concerned female officer approached her again. She bent over closer to Grace, her eyes were filled with empathy.

"You sure you don't need water?" Grace shook her head.

"You look like you will collapse any moment," she said.

Her eyes were filled with pain, tears strolled past her cheeks.

Her breathing fell erratic and everything felt dizzy. Her thoughts were interrupted by a sudden commotion. She turned around to find a furious Mr Noh with his eyes filled with tears. He walked straight to Grace and held her neck tightly as he shouted,
"You freaking murderer! You were jobless because of me and so, you killed my son? You stabbed him to death. I'm going to kill you with my own hands and avenge my son's death!"
His voice echoed in the entire police station.
Luckily the police pulled him away at the right time.
Grace stood there catching her breath, murmuring,
"I...didn't kill...Zain," her body shivered. "Please, believe me."
This increased the fury of the chairman who pounced on her again but was caught tight by a muscular officer. He shrieked,
"Sir! This is a police station, you cannot attack anyone like that."
The chairman shrugged from his hold and screamed,
"I want to see her behind the bars right now."
The officer wanted to argue when his senior stepped forward,
"Sir, don't worry. I will handle this." He ordered the cops to throw her behind the bars.

Grace sat there on the ground looking at her hands whispering,
I really didn't do anything. How can I prove myself not guilty? Who will believe me? She was suspected of murder. Thoughts started buzzing in Grace's head. *Should I call mom?*
Grace's single mother spent all her life raising her to be a successful person. Her mother worked at several restaurants just to make sure Grace could live a happy life. She was so proud of her daughter to become such a brilliant lawyer.

How could she tell her that the daughter on whom she once dotted on, the daughter who raised her head in the community, is behind the bars? That too, for murder. Her mother would face hell in the neighbourhood, for raising a murderer. As Grace was locked in thoughts, she noticed the gates of the jail opened, they screeched and shuddered. Two guards standing there informed her that she was being taken to the investigation. She stood up and walked handcuffed with the guards. She looked around, all the people in the station stared at her in disgust and apparent shock. Quick whispers were exchanged amongst the people present. She walked faster to avoid those looks passing by. She reached outside to a bigger dilemma.

She found dozens of reporters outside the station. She was frozen with shock. She moved forward putting a brave front. As soon as she stepped out, all the reporters threw endless questions at her with their mic and camera pointed at her.

"Why did you kill an innocent person?" One shouted.

"Is someone else involved with you?" Screamed another.

"Is this revenge for something?" The questions didn't stop.

"Did you murder him because he rejected you?"

"You are a lawyer yet you murdered someone, how shameful."

The disgrace went on. The crowd was pushing each other with extreme force to get an answer from her but she maintained absolute silence as she walked by.

Grace felt nauseated. She gulped the air hard and covered her mouth, bending a little.

A scream filled the place, "Is she pregnant?"

Abuses and stares deepened and news reporters started screaming many other accusations and false statements. Grace stood there with no idea of what was going on. She looked confused. She shook her head hard and tried to shout a firm no, but not even a single strand of voice came from her mouth.

Suddenly came a splashing tomato.

Then another. And another.

Grace was soaked and totally taken aback by what just happened. She saw fading angry faces in front of her demanding an explanation. Reporters clicked pictures, shouting unreasonable questions and unending abuses.

All the chaos made her lose consciousness but luckily the guards took charge of the situation, grabbed Grace and ran passing by the reporters, making it to the vehicle. Grace sat in the seat all stunned. She could barely move. She looked outside as the vehicle zoomed by the reporters.

They reached the prosecution office. It was guarded by many officers and they safely reached the place, avoiding all press. The female officer guided the handcuffed Grace into a huge hallway. There were several rooms surrounding the hall. Grace slowly passed by each mirrored room. Her nerves were shaking underneath. She soon reached a room, the female cop addressed her to sit on one of the chairs.

She looked around, scanning the area. Dozens of cameras surrounded her and a mic was placed in front of her. She sat there with closed eyes just thinking. *Why me?*

Her thoughts were interrupted by a sudden opening of the doors. She opened her eyes and sat up. She looked at the same muscular officer walking in. His uniform beamed with stars and his white turtleneck highlighted his jawline.

He looked at Grace wearily and spoke,

"Miss Grace, I am Mr Zoe the officer in charge."

His voice trailed off as he saw the condition of Grace.

She was in a complete state of trauma and drenched in tomato. Her hands still had stains of blood. Zoe went outside and requested the female officers to allow her to clean up.

When Grace came back, she was finally into a little sense. She sat on the chair opposite Zoe nervously. He gave her an assuring smile and started his round of questioning.

Zoe asked, "You are accused of murdering Zain, the successor of Noh firms, are you aware of that?"

Grace nodded nervously.

"I'll allow you to talk but first, tell me about yourself, your address and occupation and then explain the scene to me."

Grace spoke, "Officer, I am Grace. I'm a lawyer and an ex-employee of Noh-Firms. I live in Bryson Street, in Crescent Palace on the third floor. This evening I stepped out of my house to run some errands. I found my old acquaintance, Zain. I avoided him because we were on bad terms. I don't remember much but Zain followed me home during sunset. When it got darker and I did not hear his footsteps anymore, I turned back with my flashlight on. Zain had a knife pierced to his chest and behind him stood a tall man."

Zoe leaned forward, "Do you remember how he looks like?"

"No, it was very dark. Besides, he was wearing a mask. He was tall and muscular. His eyes were deep and," she paused to recollect,"...he had a scar on his neck. It was strange."

Zoe nodded as Grace continued.

"That look in his eyes. It had fear, guilt and terror all over. There was something off. He either had it planned all along or was surprised when he saw me there. Something was really off."

"Pretty observant on your part. Your statement will be recorded."

Grace nodded in agreement.

"All right, now you have two options. You can accept the investigation by my team or hire a lawyer and plead not guilty."
"But, who will take this case for me and talk against a man like Mr Noh in court?"
Zoe paused and said, "Well, then you have no option but to let the prosecution decide." "B-bu-but," Grace stammered. She didn't know what to say.

"I am sorry. But if you don't have a lawyer, we can't do much."
Grace was left in the room.
At that moment, the face of her mother flashed in front of her eyes again - toiling in the heat only to make ends meet. She imagined the warm smile on her face decked with wrinkles and tiredness. Grace trembled. She was innocent but whom should she appoint? All her fellow colleagues disliked her and she couldn't risk their career selfishly. Grace clearly knew she wasn't in a mental state to fight for herself.

"Officer, I need some time to find a lawyer. Please."
Zoe understood the situation she was in.
He thought for a while and then nodded.
"Okay. I'll allow an hour. Here's your phone. Try contacting a lawyer. Remember that you are always on surveillance so don't try unnecessary stunts. Utilize this time for the good and remember this is your last straw."

Chapter 2

Saving Grace

Her thoughts were all over the place.

What should I do? Whom do I call?

She tried remembering very hard if somebody could be of help. She never maintained contact with people in high positions. She tried thinking harder. Has she ever been in close contact with a person who can help her in this situation?

Suddenly something struck her.

Her face lit up.

Yes! Mr Hudson.

Why didn't I think of him before?

He can definitely help me out.

Her thoughts traced back to a few years. Mr Hudson was probably the most well-versed and respected lawyer of his time. He was famous for tutoring more than a hundred young students into successful lawyers with the perfect sense of justice and impartiality. Ah, those were his golden days. But he hadn't been practising in a while.

He was accused in a drug case which made him the talk of the town. It was a very controversial case and was thus picked up by the media and journals. Within a day, his dignity went down the lanes. No one turned up at the moment to help him. Grace performed some basic research on the case and knew that Mr Hudson was nowhere related to the case.

Single-handedly, Grace solved the case with complete dedication and proved the innocence of her client. Mr Hudson's happiness knew no bounds. Thanks to the disruption, he learnt an important lesson of trust that, those you think will help you, may back out and in the end, you are all alone. Mr. Hudson thanked Grace profusely. He told Grace that if at any point in her life, he could ever be of any help, Grace could contact him without any hesitation. Grace felt a ray of hope hit her. Probably, he could help her out now.

She looked at the phone and pulled up his number. She thought for a moment before clicking on the call button.

Her thoughts interrupted her. *Is it okay to ask Mr Hudson?*

Will it be too hectic for him to be pulled in this puddle of shame?

She sighed and clicked on the call button anyways, uncertain if anyone would pick up. The phone rang for a long time before a calm voice broke the silence.

"Hello? Who is this?" the voice asked.

With a nervous smile, Grace spoke on the other end.

"Mr Hudson. It's me - Grace. I worked on a case for you before. I don't know if you remember me or not, but I'm kind of in a bad situation right now." Grace took a deep breath.

There was an uncomfortable silence followed by a calm voice.

"Grace, I was hoping you would call. I saw you on TV. Don't worry, I clearly know the situation you are in. I can finally return the favour. I am too old to handle such cases, but I know the perfect person who can help. I will send him to you as soon as possible."

Grace was silenced with happiness.

She couldn't believe what she just heard.

Finally, a ray of hope in the darkness. She whispered thank you softly and her throat was soared by a sting of positiveness. Grace disconnected the call and looked at the blank walls with tears rolling back. She waited patiently. Her eyes were focused on the doors waiting for the lawyer.

Each passing moment was closer to hell. Every second of the watch reminded her of the grave destiny she would have to carry if nobody turns up. The thoughts were burdensome enough when the face of Zain hit Grace - his dimpled smile, his smirk, his voice, his rudeness, his playfulness. All the memories gushed her brain. She controlled her breath, it was heavily erratic. The thought of losing him due to her fault, though it wasn't hers, was killing her inside.

She many times wished Zain to receive his punishment, but she never thought to the extent of him being dead. Or murdered. She was lost in her thoughts which was disturbed by the opening of the door. Grace looked at the entrance with eyes filled with hope. But her eyes turned dim when Zoe appeared and sat in his chair and looked straight into her eyes.

"Grace, I have given you enough time. I am sorry," Zoe said.

Grace tried to convince him, "Please allow me a few more minutes, my lawyer will be here any moment."

Zoe said with a little disappointment, "The case will be now handed over to the prosecutor…I am sorry, Grace."

Someone knocked. Their eyes turned towards the door. A young man wearing a grey suit entered the room, with a briefcase in his hand. He had deep blue eyes and thick brown hair.

His hair was messed up, but he had an aura. The man stepped forward and said in his deep yet enchanting voice, "Who said there is no lawyer? I am the lawyer appointed for Miss Grace."

Zoe looked at Grace and then at the man. He spoke,
"I am Zoe, the investigator in charge. I will leave you alone to have a chat first."
The man smirked slightly and shook hands with Zoe.
Zoe left the room.

The man sipped the water from the glass in front of him. There was an uncomfortable silence between them. Grace looked at the man closely, he looked young and handsome. He looked more like an actor. His striking features were highly attractive but she wasn't expecting someone like him. She was expecting an old experienced man with a glow and confidence gleaming on his face, wrinkles decked due to experience - a stern lawyer. But the man sitting across her was not even the slightest of what she expected. The man finally broke the silence, he took a deep sigh and looked into her eyes.
"My name is Aiden, the lawyer sent by Mr Hudson, and I suppose you are Grace?"
Grace nodded her head.
He tilted his head, clicked his tongue and continued,
"Did you kill him?" Grace was taken aback by the question Grace replied, "No. I did not. What makes you think I did?"
Aiden saw her eyes, there was no guilt in those numb brown eyes, only uncertainty. He noticed her nails, they were crooked, indicating that she was nervous. Her legs were shaking indicating her lack of confidence. But the confidence in her voice when she said that she didn't kill Zain was certainly believable.
Aiden continued, asking a series of questions until again, silence filled the room. He closed his eyes, trying to get a hold of his thoughts. He nodded his head, submerged in thoughts and said,

"I got what I was looking for."

Grace looked at him with her eyebrows furrowed.

He laughed uncomfortably sipping his glass of water.

Grace looked at him sternly and then said,

"If this is a joke to you, please leave the case. My life is at stake here. It may be just a case to you which will probably add to your 'winning titles' or a 'loose-luck loss' but for me, it's my complete future on the line. My mother's hope for her only daughter is dependent on this case. I lost my friend, a father lost his son, a sister lost his brother, a mother lost her sunshine and a future wife lost her soulmate. But if you still think of it as just another case, you need not continue. It will hurt more to have a ray of sunshine that betrays you on a rainy day than live in complete darkness forever."

Grace just couldn't stop talking. Aiden allowed her to continue, as he knew this was her frustration talking. He sat there, quietly watching her body language, listening to what she was saying.

"It kills me when I imagine the pain of the hundreds of people who are going to miss him and if you shall make a joke out of this, please leave. I know I didn't kill him, I know I am hopeless right now and I know who I am. I don't need more pain..." her throat ached now and her voice trailed off.

Aiden was taken aback by her words. Her words were bitter but he could sense the pain behind those words. Aiden personally didn't want to act as her lawyer but these words hit him hard making this case more important. He smiled lightly and said,

"Please, Grace. Do not worry, I will give my 100% in this case."

Aiden asked Grace to continue explaining her side of the story. She narrated everything - second to second - word to word. Aiden was a bit shaken by the way she described her experience.

Grace looked up at Aiden's confused face

"What happened?"

"Something is missing, like a piece of the puzzle. Why does it sound so planned but messed up at the same time? It seems like this person wasn't actually a person in crime but just a person taken in by impulse or a person who had a completely different objective. A professional killer does not take such a risk. This case is very messed up. And to add to the mess, you were caught red-handed with a dead Zain and the knife and your fingerprints on it."

Grace laid back, "Even I think all of this is strange. But…"

Aiden nodded, "I understand. Can you please describe the man?"

Grace replied, "No, it was very dark except the faint light from my phone. All I could see were the eyes of the man. It was filled with agony, fear and anxiety. They were brownish-black. He was tall and muscular, he looked young and his face was covered by a mask."

"Any other thing which might lead us to him?"

Grace recollected the scar on his neck.

"Yes, yes there was a scar on his neck."

"A scar? That will help us filter. Anything else?"

Grace nodded lightly and exclaimed, "The roads were completely empty and due to the blackout I'm pretty sure, the cameras were out of order too."

Aiden got up in frustration and sat down again,

"You mean the roads were totally empty?"

Grace said, "Umm... As far as I remember there was no one visible at least. The roads were empty but there were some cars scattered here and there. Now I wish cars could speak."

"You wish," he snapped.

"My first step will be taking you out of this jail. I already have a plan. We have two days for the judgement. Let's try our best to collect some physical evidence till then."
Aiden took her outside followed by the guards.
Grace stopped frozen looking at the journalists.
Aiden understood the situation.

Grace tugged in her flowing shirt and gulped. Her eyes were blurred for a second. She hid behind Aiden, avoiding the quick shutters of the cameras. He caught her hand, his huge palms held the small hands of Grace in his, "Let's run Grace."
She looked at him in confusion but she followed anyway. This was her last hope to plead guilty.
They both ran at the utmost speed. As Grace ran, she felt the world walk in slow motion. She saw the reporters left behind and all she could feel was a hand clasping hers tightly.

Soon, the duo reached the van and hopped in without a second thought. Aiden looked at her trying to catch his breath. He broke out in laugher.

"Who will believe that I am a lawyer? I'm practically running with a suspect through the journalists."

Grace said panting for breath, "Thank you." and burst into pearls of laughter as well. The van started with kick-start and the prosecutor's office disappeared behind them like mist as they moved forward with speed.

It began to pour again. The roads were soon piled with utmost traffic. Aiden looked towards Grace who was looking out the window. She spoke out loud, to no one in particular.

"I have always loved the rain. It is like a symbol of freedom. They fall like stars in the day. Always played in the rain when I was young. But as I grew older, the rain became my friend whenever I was sad. I felt like I did not have to cry alone and had someone to share my tears with."

Aiden looked out and said, "True though. The clouds taught me that when it becomes harder to hold our pain inside, we should just let it out and only then we can come back to our original form. Else the pain turns into heavier, darker, black clouds carrying the weight of the world. Sometimes it's okay to let those tears drain before things get heavy. Let our hearts know, it's okay to break sometimes, you will be all right."

Grace looked at Aiden with moist eyes,

"Why are you helping me? Do you really trust me?"

Aiden said, "I came here, because of Mr. Hudson. He told me that when I was away you helped him out with a very crucial case. Of course, as of now you look guilty of this murder and you are the only suspect, but after listening to you I am sure that you be proven innocent. So, in a nutshell, I trust you and I believe you."

The rest of the journey was spent in silence. The duo reached the station soon. Aiden helped Grace hop down and then clasped her hand again taking her into the station. Aiden went straight to the head office.

Aiden spoke, "I am here for Grace," he slammed some papers on the table, "These are her papers for bail."

The officer was surprised.

He didn't quite expect a lawyer to actually turn up for Grace.

"Sir, Mr Zoe, is out due to some emergency. Once he's back, I'll ask him to give you the formalities. You may leave."

Grace was dumbstruck. She was also a law graduate, but under the pressure, she couldn't think. She looked at Aiden argue, she knew now that he was no ordinary lawyer.

Aiden and Grace walked outside the station. Grace gave out a huge gasp. She was on cloud nine. She twirled around as if the fairy of luck showered glitters from the sky on her blooded destiny.

Aiden looked at her sternly. "Grace. I just got you out of the jail. Everything is uncertain till now. Our main goal is to prove you not guilty. Let's take you back home - I'll drop you. Take rest for today, we will start the research tomorrow early morning."

Aiden dropped Grace home and she slowly walked up to her apartment. She unlocked her home. She heaved a breath of happiness. She was tear-stained. It was pitch dark in her room. She sighed. She forgot about the electrical bill. She switched on her flashlight and then went to her coffee table where she saw a note. She froze. *What's a note doing on my table?*

She picked up the note with nervousness.

Don't search for me. Or else I will get you, just like how I got Zain. Dare report this. I know your mother lives in her little comfy house near Swish Street. You wouldn't like to see her stained in blood, right? I don't think you can afford another knife stab, can you?

Her face turned pale.

She dialed Aiden.

As soon as Aiden picked up the phone, she started crying, she tried getting a hold of herself, slowly words trembled out.

"The murderer was here. He was here, Aiden. He told me that he will kill my mother and me. Please do something."

She couldn't stop crying. Aiden was worried.

He turned the car around in an instant.

"Grace, don't worry. I'm on my way, okay? Everything will be fine. Your mom will be safe. I will be there in 10 minutes and..."

Grace interrupted him, her voice shivering.

"No, I think I was wrong. He wasn't here - he is STILL here. There is someone in my room, I can feel it."

Grace breathed hard. Aiden spoke again.

"Don't move. Grace, are you listening?"

Grace was no longer listening.

Her phone dropped in terror when she felt someone in the room.

She turned back, slowly. Someone was standing behind the door.

It was the man from the murder spot.

The same eyes, the same feeling.

He whispered, "Be careful. I don't lie."

He ran at the speed of lightning.

Grace was frozen. But he had already disappeared.

She fell to the ground. She shouted in frustration.

Aiden was already there, looking at her, worry filled in his eyes.

Grace looked up. Her eyes were swollen.

"He was here. HERE. He wanted to kill my mother. He killed my friend. I will never spare him. Never EVER," she shouted.

"I missed him just by a few seconds."

She let out another shout of frustration.

Aiden bent to the ground reaching for her, "Oh my! He is a killer, Grace. What if something happened to you?"

Grace shouted, "I don't care right now. How should I calm down when that jerk has a sword over my mother's head?"

Aiden tried to calm her down and helped her to sit on a nearby bench and then brought her a warm glass of tea. As Grace slowly sipped on it, she calmed down.

"What's the matter? Why are you crying?" Aiden asked.

She replied, still sobbing, "I am the worst daughter ever. My mother worked day and night to see me happy, and me? At first, I got involved in a murder case and then, I put my mother's life in grave danger. The mother who fought the world for me."

Aiden didn't speak. He looked at her and then looked up at the stars, he said, "Your mother will be even more upset if she knew you are out here, crying, losing hope. Believe me, I will prove you innocent and we will put that murderer behind the bars."

He smiled and patted Grace's hair softly.

Grace looked at him, filled with rage driven energy,

"Yes. We will prove it. I will show the murderer what it could be if he messed with my mom."

Aiden sighed again.

He was thinking about something else.

The cold breeze turned colder, the clouds got darker indicating the chances of downpour again. Grace was slowly sipping on the tea, she was worried about what is going to happen.

"It's no longer safe for you to stay here. The murderer clearly knows your whereabouts."

Grace stood up and said with a sense of nervousness,

"That is true. But where should I go? This is all I have here and I cannot stay at a hotel. I cannot...afford it right now."

Aiden directed her towards his car and said,

"You can live at my place for a while. I have a few extra rooms. You will be safe for a few days until the culprit is caught. It is one of the safest spots for now."

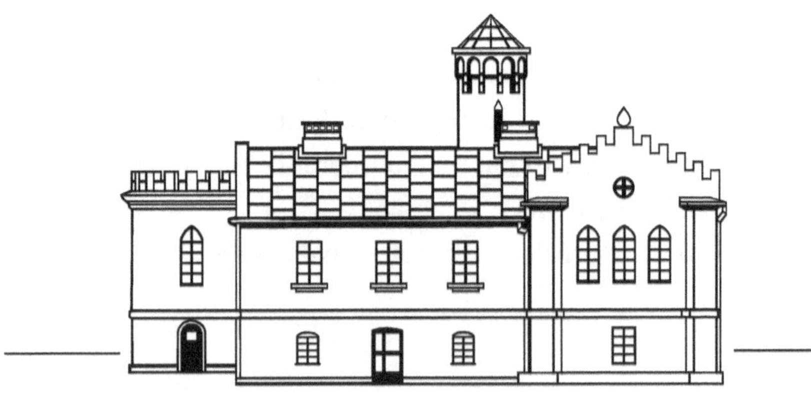

Chapter 3

Looking for Clues

Grace was a little embarrassed at first, and also a little sceptical.
Is it okay for me to follow an unknown man?
I can't be so reckless. Is it worth the risk?
But I also have no other option left.
She nodded, pushing her thoughts away.
"Alright. I'll be there in a few minutes."

Grace went upstairs, gathered her things in a bag, locked the house and left.
Aiden and Grace got into the car. The seats were comfortable. Aiden turned on some calm music and hit the road. Grace looked outside the window, there was a sense of calmness. She turned to look at Aiden. His hair was messed up by the wind and a few strands fell on his right eye, which he constantly pushed back. He had a sense of charm with a cold demeanour, like a Greek God maybe. The thought made Grace laugh.
Aiden turned his gaze towards Grace with questioning eyes.
Grace exclaimed, "Oh my! I am sorry. Just a funny thought."
Aiden smiled with a smirk and said,
"It must be about my handsome face, duh."
Grace was immediately embarrassed. *How did he know?*
Aiden replied "You are staring at me for the past few minutes. You think I wouldn't notice? Ah, but this is on me. I do have a mesmerizing face."

Grace's cheeks turned deep red, she smiled and said slyly,
"No... I wasn't really staring, I was just looking er, thinking."
She paused and turned her eyes away, "Whatever."

The conversation was interrupted by a grumbling sound.

Aiden looked at Grace. The sound came from Grace's stomach.
No Way! This unlimited embarrassment, Grace thought.
Aiden got down the car and went outside. He asked Grace to
follow. As soon as he got down, Grace hit her head. Thud
Why the heck am I being so messy today?
Aiden walked to her, "Stop hitting your head, girl. We'll need it
for the investigation. Why didn't you tell me you were hungry? I
won't charge you extra to take you to a restaurant."
Grace looked down, she whispered,
"I feel like a stupid person Aiden. I never had to depend on
someone for shelter and food."
Aiden asked her to wait there, he went to the store and got her a
cup of noodles. He handed her a cup.
"This is what I call business, madame. I help you today. You will
help me tomorrow when I call in my chit."
Aiden chuckled, Grace smiled and took a bite. It felt good.
Aiden looked at Grace, "So..."
Grace spoke, "Let's hope we can get our hands on something
good tomorrow - some hard proof."
Aiden smiled again as he took a large bite of the noodles,
"You seem hopeful. It's good."
They got in the car and within a few minutes, the car reached
outside a grand apartment. Aiden led her in. The house was huge
and it was like a palace in real life.

Aiden opened the entrance with his fingerprints and took Grace inside. The house was adorned in beautiful lights and a wooden staircase. Aiden and Grace hung their coats and moved forward. Aiden introduced the house to Grace.

"I live upstairs. There are some fruits in the kitchen if you need to eat. I usually order takeaways, so feel free to order something as well, if you're hungry. Just one thing though. Make sure it is free from any sort of mushrooms. I am highly allergic to those. If you need any help, solve it on your own. Once I fall asleep, I am as good as dead, so don't take the trouble to wake me up."

Aiden ended his huge list of instructions with a deep breath. Grace nodded reluctantly and said, "Umm! I am very good at cooking, so if you are okay with it, I can make something tomorrow. It is unhealthy to have takeaways too often."

Aiden nodded and said, "As you wish."

Grace then asked, "Actually I was curious about something."

"Do you live here all alone or somebody else lives here?"

Aiden looked a little gloomy as he said,

"I lost my parents at the age of five in a car accident in Oslo. I was raised by Mr Hudson who was my dad's best friend."

"Oh!" sighed Grace.

This explained the relation between Mr Hudson and him.

Grace and Aiden sat on a sofa as Aiden continued, grabbing a soda and passing one to Grace.

"My dad was a prosecutor and was a highly respected person in his firm. His death was a huge blow to me. He was my superhero. I wanted to follow his footsteps and decided to pursue law."

Grace noticed warm tears welling up in his eyes,

She said, "Well, nobody can understand that better than I do. My father worked as a finance director in a huge company.

There, he was falsely accused of corruption. He was shocked. He was declared a corrupt official by the media. In a few days, he died of a massive stroke. He didn't create any will so all the property was taken by his elder brother. It was disheartening for my mother. I mean, how would she manage a 6-year old all by herself with hardly any money? She worked hard to educate me. So, I decided to pursue law, to not let anyone face a situation like my father. This is also why I helped Mr Hudson. He is such an amazing person. It was obvious he was being framed so I took the risk and It paid off."

Aiden smiled. It was nice to finally have someone to talk to.

"But, why did you agree to help me? For Mr Hudson?"

Aiden took a deep sigh. He flipped his hair back and laid back on the sofa, "I told you, it was for Mr Hudson. Also, this case was very interesting." He yawned, "It is late. We have an early day."

Grace stood up and walked towards her room. She lay on her bed. It was comfortable. In a few minutes, she fell asleep.

The next morning, Grace woke up early, took a shower and headed straight to the kitchen. She made some sandwiches, pancakes and brewed two cups of coffee. In a while, Aiden came jogging down the stairs and was surprised to see a full table. They sat down and ate, chatting and laughing. It was after years he ate a home-cooked meal. Aiden sipped on his coffee.

"Better than Starbucks" he said. "Let's go?"

They left home a couple of hours after sunrise.

Aiden pulled over at the store where Grace met Zain.

He flashed his ID at the shopkeeper.

"I need the CCTV footage of the shop from yesterday, please."

The man recognized Grace. He shrugged and looked at Aiden.

"Sir, due to the blackout, the CCTV outside wasn't working. But I have the footage from the inside as it is connected to backup power. Will that work?" He scanned Grace with judging eyes.

"Thank you. We need the footage roughly from around 5:30 to 6 PM," said Grace to the man who exchanged a piercing glance.

The shopkeeper turned the large desktop towards the two of them. Aiden skimmed through the entire footage and looked at Grace in frustration.

"Are you crazy? You picked up coffee, noodles and went straight to a knife? The tension between you two is clearly visible. Additionally, the knife here does not help," he frowned.

"Why were you looking at the knife so weirdly?"

"Well, the last knife I brought broke into two within a year. I needed to ensure it is worth the price."

Aiden was about to close it when suddenly Grace intervened. She saw a man wearing black, walking slyly on the reflection of the store's mirror. She paused the recording and clicked a photo.

"This is him. This is definitely him." Aiden zoomed in and smirked. They finally took the first step of proving her not guilty. There was hope. Aiden thanked the shopkeeper and walked out of the shop. The murder scene was just up ahead. It was covered in yellow tape and guarded by the officials.

Aiden thought to himself. The photo can be a good lead, but it cannot be presented as evidence. Aiden asked Grace to show him her house and lead her to where the murderer stood yesterday.

The duo was now in front of the apartment. She always locked her place. *How did he get in?* Grace never took the time to find out how he broke into her house in the first place. They rushed inside for clues. It was a tiny house with just a room and a kitchen as small as a closet.

Aiden searched the room. He needed something that would add another piece to the puzzle. She checked the window and banged on it in frustration. A cold breeze touched her skin, sending shivers down her spine.

Ah! There was a crack. Someone had tampered with it.

She shouted, "Aiden! Aiden! Check this out."
"Holy Moly," he whispered under his breath. He pulled the window straight up and bent down to see where it led. He saw a pipe running down. It was strong and stiff, good enough to hold up a human. He gulped, slowly climbed down the window. In a few seconds, he disappeared. Grace could no longer see him. "Aiden? Are you there?"

Chapter 4

The Black Tank

"Hey. Stop shouting. I am right here. Just climb down."
Aiden's voice echoed. Grace shouted again anyway.
"Are you nuts? No way."
"Grace, please. Stop playing around. Come down. NOW!"
He sounded dangerous. Grace climbed down the pipe.
Soon she noticed that there was a cement platform just a few steps below. She jumped onto that and saw Aiden standing there.
"Good work! I thought I would see you tumbling down."
He turned his gaze around to see what place this was. A similar pole caught his eyes.
"There, That could be our next clue. What is that place?"
"I have no idea." She scanned the area.
"Wait…that floor is empty for a long time. An old man used to live there but he moved out a couple of months ago."
"All right what are we waiting for then?"

Grace smacked his arm. "If you expect me to climb that and fall to my death, you are crazy. You may be a daredevil, I am not."
Aiden took her hand and sprinted anyway. She screamed but it was too late. They were already on the first step. She shivered
"Grace, trust me, okay?" Aiden wrapped his arms around her.
"There is a huge foot space here. You won't fall. I promise."
Grace looked up at him and stepped up. She felt confident. She moved forward. They both managed to get onto the rooftop.

In front of them was a gate. They tried to open it but in vain.

Bang! Bang! The sound echoed through the streets.

Grace started panicking, "What should we do now? If the murderer shows up, he will kill both of us." Grace stepped back and looked around for something that could help them get in.

Something else caught her attention. There was a peculiar scent lingering on the terrace. She saw a black tank in the corner. She left Aiden alone and moved towards the tank. Something about it was off. She examined the tank carefully. Grace looked at the platform the tank stood on.

Why is there mud on the bottom of the platform?

She bent down to touch the mud. It had a semi-rough structure.

On examining closer, Grace's eyes widened in shock.

Red stains covered the platform.

The peculiar stink now hit her harder.

She shrieked in terror.

Aiden rushed to her.

"What happened to you? Are you okay?"

Grace shivering, pointed towards the tank.

Aiden looked at the tank and then towards Grace.

Grace nervously whispered, "Blood! There is blood!"

Aiden moved a little forward and bent to find bloodstains on the tank. The tank was pitch black but the bottom stone had dark red stains on them. He lifted the cover of the tank to expose the deadly smell of rotten bodies. The smell was toxic and at the same time intolerable. He covered his nose. Grace coughed.

Aiden guessed it was rats as the building was abandoned.

Grace felt uncomfortable looking at the frozen Aiden.

She stammered, "What is in it?" He did not reply.

Aiden stood there looking at the tank with no movement.

Slowly, Grace moved forward to peek inside.
She squealed and fell to the back.
Aiden turned back, to see Grace on the ground shivering. Aiden was dumb-struck too. He bent again and saw inside the tank.
The dead stink was not of rats or any other animal.
It was of a human. A dead corpse.

The tank was not very deep. It was just a few inches and was completely dry. The corpse lay right at the base of the tank. With shivering fingers, Aiden dialed the police station.
"Hello? There is an emergency here. There is a corpse in a tank here at Bryson Street..." Aiden's voice trailed off.
A shivering Grace hugged her knees.
She could not erase the image from her mind.

A few minutes later, the police arrived.
They broke through the front gate and rushed above.
They found Aiden and Grace by the black tank.
The spot was instantly investigated by the officers and a few forensic reporters. The police questioned the duo. Aiden answered most of the questions since Grace was in an utter state of shock. She watched as the body was being pulled out and packed into a black bag. The police sealed the area and escorted Aiden and Grace downstairs. They handed them a bottle of water and continued their questioning.
Once they left, Aiden looked at Grace with concern.
"Are you okay?"
Grace said, "I am not sure. Did you look at the body? The rotten stink means it was killed only a few days ago. The face... seemed so familiar. I have seen this man somewhere. But where?"

Grace tried to focus when Aiden interrupted,

"Grace? Don't think about all this. We have the court session the day after tomorrow. We need to focus on what is important."

Aiden and Grace walked towards the car. It was almost midnight. They both were taken aback by all that had happened.

The day was exhausting.

If it was the same murderer, why did he choose the terrace?

It could be possible that he left from there and locked the gate.

What if both of them were two different killers?

All these thoughts clouded them.

Aiden tried to make Grace feel at ease. She herself was trying to stay calm and gather her thoughts. Aiden started the car, there was silence. The silence was interrupted by a sudden phone call.

Grace saw the phone. She froze.

It was an unknown number...

"Put it on speaker," Aiden said. His eyes were assuring.
Grace felt protected. She picked up the phone
"Hello? Who is this?"
"Are you kidding me, Miss Grace?"
Grace gasped. She took off the phone from the speaker.
"Mom! Hey. How are you?"
"Hey? My foot. You are under murder suspicion. The least you could do was call me."
"Mom. I am sorry, I didn't want to worry you. Don't worry about me. I have a friend here, er, his name is Aiden. He is helping me out with it. He is my lawyer. I am not going to jail, okay?"
"You better not. Take care of yourself. I'll come, see you soon."
Grace smiled. She continued, "Thank Aiden for me."
"Okay, mom. Bye. I love you." Grace hung up.
Aiden looked at her and let out a chuckle."

As soon as they reached, Grace went straight to her room and took a shower. She put on her pyjamas and headed to the kitchen.

She made pasta for dinner. Aiden helped her do all the chopping. It felt nice to cook and do something for himself. He felt cared for and important.

"Thank you. Aren't you tired? We could've ordered pizza."
"For all that you are doing for me, this is barely anything."
They smiled, trying to push all the thoughts of the evening away.

It was morning already.

Tiny streaks of sunlight were hushing down the windows of Grace's room. She rose up and stretched her arms, it was calm and peaceful. Grace made two cups of coffee and waited for Aiden. She decided to make a salad. She headed to the fridge to find a yellow sticky note on it. Grace pulled it out and read it.

Morning, Grace. I am sorry but I have to head out somewhere due to some work. I will see you in court tomorrow morning. Mr Hudson will pick you up from here.

Grace was a little unhappy. The hearing was tomorrow and there was no proper proof with them yet. Aiden prioritized something or *someone* over her. She was frustrated. She lost her appetite.
She tapped the breakfast island nervously. She decided to explore the house. She walked to the study room. The room was very huge, just like an indoor library. Grace looked around, there were nearly a dozen shelves full of books. The study table in the corner overflowed with papers and files. Grace rummaged through the books. The books were mostly of the non-fiction genre or were of crime fiction. Aiden seemed to keep his books clean and neat.

Grace kept moving around when she saw a photo of Aiden with a boy. Both of them in the picture looked young - maybe in their teens. The other was tall, handsome, pale and looked very smart. *Who is he?* thought Grace.

She was bored now. She went to the living room and played a movie on the TV.

Hours went by. Grace put on another movie. Time seemed to fly. Grace was trying to pay attention to the movie but her mind wandered. *Where was Aiden? Who is that boy in the picture?*

Aiden stood in front of a photo. He was wearing a black suit with a few roses in his hand. His eyes were tear-stained, but he maintained a smile on his face.

"Lucas. I have not visited you for a long time, right? I am sorry. I have been busy with cases piling up. I have missed you a lot. Do you know, I met someone? She reminds me of you. She is sweet. She frustrates me sometimes, but she's kind. I am helping her prove her innocence in a murder case. Lucas, without you, I am really incomplete. I hope you were stronger that time…."

Aiden's voice trailed off.

The tears held within for years came streaming down his face. But each falling pearl made him stronger. He needed to vent. He hugged the photo, placed the flowers and walked out.

He sat on the stairs quietly, alone with his thoughts.

His mind raced back to the time he was alive, six years ago.

Life was perfect, Aiden and Lucas were best friends. They knew each other since childhood and shared everything with each other. They were all they had.

But then, Aiden moved to Australia for a year.

Everything was okay initially. They spoke to each other every day. The bond was deeper, to be honest. The distance between where they lived could not distance their friendship.

Aiden flew back to America and drove to Lucas to surprise him. His memories were fresh like yesterday. It was snowing heavily the day he returned and reached Lucas's house. It was quiet. Aiden rang the bell a few times. The sound echoed but no one answered. He opened the door using the key they usually hid under the plant. He went inside calling for Lucas. No one was home. He reached his bedroom. What he saw next horrified him.

His best buddy was entangled in a rope. Aiden fell pale. He never expected his friend, who taught him smiling would be hanging on a fan, breathing his last.

Aiden fell to the ground crying, shouting and shocked. He could not believe his eyes. He was in denial for the next few minutes. He later got to know that, Lucas was falsely accused of being a bully in his new university. No longer being able to take all the hatred, Lucas ended his life. The desperation in his eyes to prove himself innocent shook Aiden to his core.

He saw the same desperation in Grace's eyes.

When Mr Hudson offered him such cases, he denied them. But this time, he fought the case, for Lucas, for himself and for his father. Each time Aiden looked at the picture of Lucas, it reminded him how a smiling face could have thousands of swords pierced in. Each time Aiden thought about giving up, Lucas' smiling face flashed in front of his eyes. The eyes which signaled him to keep fighting - to not give up as he did. Probably, the bravest people on the outside turn to be hurting on the inside.

The thoughts of Aiden were interrupted by two men arguing.
The first man shouted, "You hit my car!"
The other man rebelled back, "It wasn't my fault."
The first man yelled in frustration, "Do you have any proof?"
The man grinned and said, "Dashcam. That's my proof."
The first man fell silent and left.
The second man boarded his car and left humming.

Aiden looked at the two cars leaving. He found another piece that seemed hopeful, but would it fit in this puzzle of stained destiny?

His thoughts were interrupted by a familiar voice.

"Aiden! Get in, I got the appointment of the forensic doctor."

Rolling his eyes, Aiden got in the car and faced that person,

"I owe you this. Let's go now. We'll do a quick analysis."

It was nearly sunset. Grace was fed up watching television and reading. She opened her phone and scrolled her social media feed. She saw something shocking. There were many posts and articles about her. She was being trolled by thousands of fans. She was being abused without mercy. Grace was shocked as well as frustrated. Without any proof, she was declared as guilty of a murder she never did. She was terrified. She threw herself on her bed, her eyes were numb and her body was aching. She was disappointed. She felt like crying but her tears had already dried. She was waiting for the sun to rise.

Tomorrow will decide her destiny.

She sat by the window, she had lost her appetite.

Will the right win or circumstances?

In life, right people face wrong circumstances.

What happens then?

Grace wanted to share her pain with someone but she was miserably alone. For the first time, she wanted to rely on someone but there was no one. She rolled on her bed. After getting dragged into such a big case who will hire her? Zain was a famous idol and his dad has a reputation in the law world. Grace gathered her thoughts and tried to focus on the positives. She fell asleep in a few minutes.

The sun was barely shining, the clouds were thick and heavy winds were flowing. A black day indeed. Grace pulled herself out of the bed. It was the day of the hearing. She rushed inside the bathroom, had a shower and put on her grey formals with a white lining. She went out to the hall. To her surprise, Aiden was back already neatly dressed in his black suit and a grey tie. Aiden looked tired. He was sitting on the couch with his eyes closed. It was clear that he barely had enough sleep.

Aiden sensed Grace was there. "Good Morning! I will just take a power nap, go ahead and eat something. There are some muffins and sandwiches - don't overwork yourself today."

Grace sat on the sofa next to him. She sighed. She wanted to ask him about finding evidence, but Aiden's face showed clear signs of dismissal. Grace was sure that probably there was no clue for her to be set free. By now, Grace was mentally prepared and ready to depart from the kind care she was living.

Aiden was already half asleep. His face was pale and his body tired. Grace touched his forehead. It was burning hot! Grace stood up in anxiety, she pulled out a thermometer from the shelf and checked his temperature. It was 102 degrees F. She panicked. She rushed inside the kitchen with some wet napkins and put them on his forehead, gently. The temperature seemed to increase. She was worried. "Aiden you are burning hot," she said. Aiden smiled half-consciously, "I know! I am perfectly hot." Grace rolled her eyes at his joke and clicked her tongue.

She remembered she had some pills in her first aid.

She rushed to get a tablet.

"Why didn't you tell me? Here take this tablet."

"What are you doing? I will be sleepy if I take tablets now.

It is already 8 AM. We have to be there by 9:30. It's a Monday.
There will be heavy traffic. Let's leave now."
Aiden tried to get up but fell down back due to fatigue.
Grace helped him sit behind comfortably,
"Aiden, you can't go. You are sick."
"Sick? No way. It is just tiredness." He was simply unbelievable.
"Do you want all our work to go down the drain? Never," he said.

Aiden got up again. Grace helped him reach the car.
She grabbed the keys and said, "I will drive."
"I hope I reach there alive," Aiden murmured.
"You know, I don't really sympathise with sick people."
Aiden stopped smiling, his eyes spoke a lot.
Grace smiled, "I was joking. Don't worry about today."
"Everything will be alright. Even if it doesn't go too well, you need not blame yourself. Sometimes it's all about the fate and destiny written in heaven."
Grace looked at Aiden with eyes of assurance, she turned her eyes to the road and bit her lower lip. *I hope it goes well.*

The duo reached the court at the right time. It was extremely crowded since it was. Journalists and young fans hovered the place waiting for either side of the lawyer to appear.
Aiden was dumbstruck, he expected a crowd but not in this number. He wondered what to do. He then said,

"Grace! stop the car by the path on the side. It is not safe here."
Grace stopped the car by the aisle.
Aiden picked up his phone and dialled a few numbers weakly,
"Hello, uncle. Yes, we are here but..." he paused.
"Oh? Okay. Thank you so much."
Aiden asked Grace to come out and said,
"Let's go. Uncle Hudson is waiting for us at the back entrance."
Aiden and Grace quietly strolled past and rushed to the back gate.
It was empty. Mr Hudson was nowhere to be seen.
"Uncle?" shouted Aiden.
"Shh! Here! Come here."

They heard a shadow on the nearby staircase.
They followed the voice instantly.
An old man in his fifties stood there with a warm smile, his hair
had more pepper than salt. Beside him, stood a tall and handsome
man. He had silk blonde hair and charming deep brown eyes. His
smile was dazzling and there was a charm on his face.
"Hello, Grace. Long time," Mr Hudson spoke.
He shook Grace's hands with delight. Grace smiled brightly,
"Director Hudson. Umph, I am sorry - Mr Hudson. It is such a
pleasure to see you. Thank you, sir."

Mr Hudson chuckled,

"Oh please. It was nothing to what you did."

Grace looked at the man with no identity, "And he is?"

The man shook her hand,

"Hello! My name is Alan, the son of Mr Hudson and I'm a best friend and kind of a cousin to the lawyer here," he pointed towards Aiden. "I have been helping Aiden with the case."

"Hello, Alan. I am Grace. I am so thankful for your help…"

she was interrupted by Aiden,

"Best friend? Wow!" he said sarcastically.

"You were never my friend. You left me all alone when I was 13 and returned back from Australia last month. You think I will forgive you, you abandoner?"

Aiden complained childishly. Alan chuckled slightly.

Grace said to Alan, "Please don't mind him, he doesn't mean it."

Aiden whispered, "Wow! People change all of a sudden."

Grace nudged Aiden with her elbow, "Shut it, will you?"

Aiden growled in pain and then laughed. He straightened his crooked tie, took a deep sigh and said, "All right, let's go."

Chapter 5

Judgement Day

Grace was seated on the wooden table. Next to her was Aiden and Alan. She almost bawled out when she saw her mother in the courtroom, eyes filled with worry. On seeing Grace, her mother instantly sent her assuring messages through her eyes. Aiden looked at her mother and nodded to greet her.

After a while, Aiden whispered, "The judge will be here any moment, try your best to look confident and don't look so tense."

"Yeah, Sure. Are you okay? Are you still hot?"

Aiden whispered back, "I was always hot, Miss Grace."

Grace looked at him with disgust, "Give it a break, Mr Lawyer."

Alan chuckled. He was certainly enjoying this.

Grace looked around, she whispered,

"Where is the investigation team? I haven't seen them since the day of the investigation. Have they conducted any investigation to begin with?"

"I assumed Mr Zoe was a pretty efficient officer, but his negligence has really pierced me. He isn't at fault either. Mr Noh has his own ways of threatening people to leave things alone."

The chairman, Mr Noh soon arrived. He looked stern and extremely cold. Grace's eyes widened. She touched her neck remembering their last meeting at the police station. Aiden noticed it and held her hand. It felt warm, Grace wasn't scared any longer. She wrapped her little fingers around his palm and rubbed her thumb to his palm bone. Her heart was pounding hard. She whispered to herself, *God, I'm at the stake of living or dying. Can my heart stop fluttering so crazily just because of a guy's sweaty hands? It is so silly and immature*

The chairman sat on the other end of the room with his lawyer, Mr Stank. The lawyer looked very confident and calm. He kept looking at Grace, which certainly hit her confidence. Alan noticed Aiden holding her hand. He smiled. He could sense the chemistry between them. His dear friend was learning to love, care and cherish again.

His thoughts were broken by the entry of the judge. All the people present in the room rose as soon as the judge entered. The judge seated and ordered the prosecution to begin.

Mr Stank: "Your honour, Mr Zain, the heir to Noh Firms was murdered last Friday, by the chief suspect, who is also an old frenemy of Zain, Miss Grace. We want to charge life-long imprisonment for her to reflect on her mistakes."

Aiden stood up to speak, "Your honour. We plead not guilty."

The judge asked them to continue and present their points.

Mr Stank stood up and called Grace to the witness box.

Grace walked straight to the box and stood there, she bowed to the judge and looked at the lawyer.

Mr Stank: "Miss Grace, last Friday, did you meet Zain, right before he was murdered?"

Grace nodded. "Yes, it is true but…" Grace was interrupted.

Mr Stank: "No buts. Just answer my question."

The lawyer slammed the box in anger.

"Objection, your honour," said Aiden.

Grace was scared.

She flinched and shivered slightly.

Aiden was furious, he nearly got up from his seat, but Alan stopped him.

"Not now. Remember, we're in the courtroom."

Aiden sat back in frustration. His fever was already at peaks and the rough behaviour of the lawyer was rising his peace levels.

Mr Stank: "Miss Grace! Would you deny the fact that you and Zain always fought with each other?"

Grace bit her lips, she knew she was doomed.

Looking at quiet Grace, the lawyer smirked,

"You don't want to accept? Fine. You may now go back."

Grace trembling sank back to her seat.

The lawyer called upon one of the colleagues of their office in the witness box. The young man blurted out, "Yes, it is obviously true. The two fought all the time. They also ignored each other. After Grace left the office, she would curse him in public as well and threaten that she will finish him."

Mr Stank: "Please note that, court. Mentally abusive wars and open warnings"

Grace: "No. I really didn't...kill him."

Judge: "Speak only when questioned."

Grace felt numb. She was blank.

The world was spinning for her.

The lawyer looked at Aiden with eyes glowing with power and superiority. Aiden avoided his eye contact. He was much more nervous than he looked. The lawyer now called upon the shopkeeper. The rough man came in the box and bowed.

Mr Stank: "Sir, Please describe what you saw that day."

Shopkeeper: "The lady came to my shop that day. It had been raining all day, the sun had just set and there was a blackout. She purchased coffee, noodles and a knife. She usually purchases all these items from my store. Just then, a tall, muscular guy entered the shop and tried to speak to her but she told him to get lost.
She looked really angry. She also pointed the knife towards him but I warned her that it was too sharp. They walked out of the shop. A few minutes later, I heard a shriek. I ran outside to see. I saw that lady and that tall guy. She had the knife in her hands and the tall guy was dead."

Mr Stank: "Your honour. Do note. Open warnings, purchasing a knife and the cold revenge between them. Isn't it too much of a coincidence? I have submitted the forensic reports to you. Zain was stabbed to death and the knife has fingerprints of Grace on them. On top of that, the only witness has seen Zain with Grace decked in blood."
There were rushed and tensed murmurings in the court.
Aiden walked to the witness box. "What was your first reaction looking at the scene?" Shopkeeper: "I was numb and shocked."
Aidem: "Why did you fall numb?"
Shopkeeper: "Sir, you must be joking. It was a murder. At such a sight, anyone could topple their senses right away."
Aiden: "Exactly. Any normal person would lose their senses. That is what happened to my client. You can check with the local police about her state when they saw her. A killer would sprint or act sly. She was completely shocked. Grace just saw her friend soaked in blood, she rushed over to him and removed the knife with an intention of saving him but unfortunately, the wound was too deep. Zain was killed in a few seconds"

Mr Stank: "There is no proof of what you are trying to say.

Aiden requested Mr Noh to come in the box.

Aiden: "Sir, just like your lawyer stated, my client gave open warnings and abuses. Do you think she literally means it?"

Mr Noh: "Yes, that rotten egg had all intentions of ending my son!"

Aiden: "First of all, watch your language. You are in a courtroom. Secondly, didn't you rush over to the police station and instantly try to kill Grace? You caught her neck and shouted that you will murder her. Didn't you?"

Mr Noh: "Th-Tha-That was out of grief. How could I, a person like me get as lowly as murdering someone?"

Aiden smirked: "So your emotions are emotions. Your use of vocabulary is literature and my client's is an attempt to murder?"

Grace felt her eyes welling up, she could see the dedication of Aiden and the hard work he has put in. She was proud of him.

Mr Noh: "This girl, she...she is capable of murdering anyone."

Aiden took a minute to breathe and get a hold of his emotions.

He got back to the witness box and argued further.

Aiden: "You knew she was capable of murder, yet you employed her? You also gave her the award for being the best employee of the year. Isn't it true that you ignited their fights just because she brought you fame and success? You still say she is capable of murdering someone but you allowed your son to chase her? Tell me, what kind of a father allows his son to date a murderer?"

He paused, as if for dramatic effect and continued,

"You are very well aware of the illegal matters your son was involved in before."

Mr Noh was at a loss for words now.

The lawyer of Noh stood up and said,

"Objection, your honour."

Judge: "Objection overruled. Go ahead, Mr Aiden."

Aiden: "Thank you, sir."

He took a deep sigh and called upon the forensic doctor.

"Can we please hear your result of the investigation?"

Doctor: "I have been working on this case and there are some major points missed that I want to share. Firstly, two knives were brought to the lab. The first one is the knife from which Mr Zain was murdered and the second one was from Miss Grace's bag. Both the knives are of different qualities and sizes. So it is impossible for her to use the knife she purchased at the grocery store to cause such a deep wound. Also, Miss Grace could not have stabbed him as the stab wound was deep. She would have to be a trained fighter to inflict such a deep wound with an ordinary knife. This is a wound that can be caused by someone taller and stronger. The force applied was extremely high and it resulted in the tearing of the muscle tissue right away."

Grace sighed. Thankfully someone else also was in her favour. Aiden bowed and sat back in his seat. His breathing was tensed and erratic. There was murmuring in the room with surprised glances. Grace's mother gave out a breath of relief.

The judge looked upon all the files provided to him and looked with questioning eyes towards Mr Noh. The chairman had already skunked his head down. Mr Stank stood up again.

Mr Stank: "Sir are you sure about Grace not being able to cause the wound? I have heard that when people are mad with rage, they do things unexpectedly stronger."

The doctor was lost in his thoughts for a while and said,
"Sir, this is just my hunch, the wound is too deep to be caused by someone shorter than Mr Zain's height. But as you said, sometimes things may go unexpected."
Mr Stank: "Your honour, clearly according to the shopkeeper, he saw Zain in the arms of Grace. I don't think if we will require more detailed evidence. Also, the investigation of the doctor is just a hunch, not based on evidence."

Aiden looked at Grace, his eyes filled with fatigue, Grace was lightly tear-stained, she nodded her head telling him to relax.
Mr Stank: "Your honour, All the evidence presented by the defence till now were purely literary. There is no physical evidence to prove Grace is not guilty. We have a witness who claims to have seen the after-murder scene, I don't think there is any other evidence required."

The judge nodded to the statement of the lawyer. He slowly removed his spectacles and stared in blank space for a while.

Everybody in the court looked straight at the judge waiting for his announcement. Aiden went through his documents to find a loophole, but it seemed like a checkmate. He was feeling furious and hopeless. He felt his body turn hotter and his vision turning dazed. He tried grabbing consciousness, but sparks of headache hit his forehead, he was falling numb. He looked towards the Judge who was busy going through the documents. His eyes slowly wandered towards Grace who was looking at her mother exchanging worried conversations through glances.

For the first time, Aiden felt useless.
It looked like he was failing.

He thought the doctor's statement was an opening, but it turned out to be a miserable dead-end.

The sound of a ringing bell filled the room.

The judge finally spoke, "The court is adjourned till tomorrow."

Grace flinched on hearing the ringing bell, she sighed happily. Aiden took a calm breath and collected his papers. His eyes were red with dissatisfaction and guilt.

Grace looked at Aiden and whispered,

"It's okay, you must be really tired. I got a day to say goodbye." Grace smiled harder deepening her dimple. There was a smile on her face but her eyes were filled with remorse and sadness. Grace found herself stained in tears. She had the chance to prove herself innocent but she failed. Aiden took a step away from Grace but then, his vision blurred. Everything started fading away. Things started going up and down and then suddenly he found himself on the cold floor.

A huge thud echoed through the half-empty courtroom.

Chapter 6

Is This the End?

Everything went numb for Grace.
She shrieked, "Aiden!"

Grace rushed over beside him falling on her knees. He lay there, looking lifeless. He wasn't moving an inch. Grace touched his forehead, it was like a blazing piece of coal.
Alan whispered, "Let us get out of here. The journalists will be swarming any moment. We can't take him to the hospital given the situation. Let's take him home."
Grace nodded reluctantly. Alan picked Aiden up in his arms and rushed outside. He stopped a few feet away from the gate. The journalists were huge in number. It was impossible to reach the back entrance without crossing them.
Grace stood there lifeless. *What should we do now?*
At that moment, Mr Hudson walked outside. All the journalists jumped forward shovelling mics asking questions. It was the best distraction for the journalists. Alan took the opportunity and raced to the back door followed by Grace. Alan reached the basement and started the car. Grace sat on the backseat and Alan placed fainted Aiden on her lap. He zoomed.
Grace looked down on Aiden, he was burning with fever.
He had spent the whole night, preparing for the session today.
She whispered. "This is all my fault."

Alan turned back with concerned eyes,

"Grace, Don't cry. It isn't your fault. He is a workaholic. Besides, he did it for you. How do you think will he feel looking at you smudged in tears?"

Grace looked at herself in the mirror, her cheeks were flushed and her eyes were deep red from crying. Her hair was sticking out. She wiped her running nose and nodded lightly. She kept her eyes focused on Aiden. She caressed his hair gently. Softly, she rubbed her hand on his fluffy, silky hair.

She bent and whispered in Aiden's ears,

"Please don't hurt yourself. I can't imagine the world without you anymore." She pulled her head back.

Grace did not shift her eyes from Aiden.

Within a few minutes, the car stood in front of the huge mansion. Alan zoomed forward and half-parked the car. He jumped to the back gate and gave a piggyback ride to Aiden.

Grace hurriedly unlocked the gate.

"Alan, take him to my room, I will be there in a few minutes."

Alan rushed inside the room and laid Aiden on the bed. Aiden still laid there without moving. Grace reached there with a bowl of cold water and a cloth. She sat down beside Aiden and instantly sprinkled some water on his face, Aiden's eyes twitched but he lay there without moving.

Grace whispered,

Thank god, his eyes just moved.

Once his temperature drops, he will wake up.

Alan went outside the room leaving Grace alone with Aiden. Grace took out a thermometer and checked, it was nearly 104°F She gasped and gripped a fever-relief pill. She put the pill in his mouth and helped him gulp down some water.

Aiden gulped the water in half-consciousness.
Grace controlled her tears from falling again.
She undressed his coat and threw it on the nearby table.
She unbuttoned his collar so he could breathe better.
Now he'll feel a little better, she thought.
She opened the windows to let cold breezes in.

There was a calm silence in the room. She stared at the sleeping figure of Aiden. He was masculine and had his muscles popped from his shirt. His abs were slightly visible through the opened buttons and his soft lips crawled and curled in discomfort. His huge hand wrapped around Grace as hard as possible. His hair was all messed up and he looked a little uncomfortable due to the high fever.

Grace wiped his forehead, her light pink lips touched the forehead of Aiden, She rose up and walked outside. She saw Alan sitting worried on the sofa. Grace placed her hand on his shoulder and said, reassuringly,
"Alan, Aiden's fever will come down in a while. Thank you for your help. I will leave now."

Alan was concerned, "But where will you go?"
"I will go home for now. Tomorrow is a tough day."
Alan wanted to stop her and say something but he couldn't.
"Bye, if I stay longer, I wouldn't be able to leave. Thank you for everything. Please stay with him and take care of him for me."

She walked straight outside without turning back.
She slammed the door behind her and took out a huge sigh.

I will never see you again. I am so sorry, Aiden. Bye.

Grace called for a taxi and sat down on the back seat. Tears started strolling down her cheeks as she saw the huge mansion disappear into the misty air.

She never thought that a person will become so important to her in just a couple of days. She consoled herself. *No, Grace. You did the right thing. You cannot risk his life, because the journey is going to get tougher.*

Soon, she found the car reach the street.

She hopped outside and walked straight into the apartment.

It was very chilly and cold breezes hit like arrows in the sky.

Aiden seemed to recover - thanks to the medicine.

Aiden got up flinching, he screamed, "Grace?"
Alan was happy to see him awake, "You finally woke up, your fever seems to have gone and look the way you are sweating. Your shirt is dead wet."
Aiden looked around and nodded absent-mindedly,
"I feel better, but where is Grace?"
Alan looked lost, "Um..." *What should I say?*
Aiden raised his eyebrow, "Where is she?"
Alan gave up looking at his desperate face, "Grace left."
"Left?" Aiden screamed, "Where?"
Alan tried to avoid eye contact,
"She said she doesn't want to put you in danger, so she decided to leave for her home."

Aiden's grey eyes widened, he shook his head.
He sat there without moving an inch.
He jumped and ran straight to the door.
His body was still weak and his sight was still blurred.

Alan shouted, "Your fever just came down."
He chased him. "Where are you going?"
Aiden yelled, "The murderer knows the location of Grace perfectly. One small ignorance and he may kill Grace. He knows where she lives. He has his chance..." Aiden's voice trailed.

His breath was uneven, bad thoughts gushed in one by one.
Alan followed him and caught him by his shoulder.
He shrieked, "I will drive."

Aiden nodded and jumped to the passenger seat.

The duo rushed through the roads to the street where Grace lived. Aiden closed his eyes and opened the windows, he still felt dizzy but nothing mattered more than losing Grace. He heaved a deep breath. *Why did you leave me? For me, the biggest danger is you being alone right now. How will I deal with life if you'll be gone?* The arrows of breezes shot a tear right in the air flying across. Aiden pulled his head back and let two more drops of cold tears fall down his cheeks. Alan looked at Aiden with pity.

Grace walked inside her building and climbed the steps. She reached outside the door. She tried to look happy as it was her last day at home but she missed Aiden. While unlocking the door, she saw something lying next to her door. It was a beautiful blue wrapped box. Grace furrowed her eyebrows, *Who sent these?*

She saw that there was a black rose on it.
The flower looked extremely pretty.
Grace put it aside and started unwrapping.

Maybe some co-worker must have sent this as a farewell gift.
She saw that there was a wooden box underneath it.
The packaging looked lovely.

After opening the wooden box, her brown pupils expanded, her face lost the color, she turned pale. She didn't move an inch, everything turned blurred. She fell down on her knees, the box fell with a thud on the ground. She couldn't speak. She closed her eyes and pushed herself to the wall. She looked down and caught her head, her head sunk between her knees. She finally was able to scream filled with desperation, anger, fear and frustration.

Her voice echoed in the whole building.
Aiden and Alan were on the stairs to the building.
On hearing the scream, Aiden looked all pale.

He jumped one step to another to reach Grace within a few seconds. Alan paced up and reached the floor. Aiden saw Grace lying beside her door with her head in her hands weeping uncontrollably. He saw a box on the floor, he peeked at it to find something disgusting.
The box had a dead mouse with a photo of Grace stained in red. He turned his gaze away instantly. He could feel the pain Grace was feeling. He jumped on his knees and tried to hold her.
Grace flinched in fear and tried to push the hand away.

Aiden held her tighter and whispered, "It's just me, Grace."
Grace lifted her eyes and looked at him. Her eyes were red and her nose was running. Her hair was strangled and her face was flushed.
"I am sorry, I am late," Aiden said
Grace sobbed harder, "I am scared, Aiden."
Both of them sat there for a while.
He shuddered on the thought,
What could have happened if he were late?
Grace looked so scared and was in complete trauma.

Alan instantly threw the box in disgust.

The clouds were turning black.

Thunder and a loud clamming sound echoed through the place.

Grace flinched slightly.

"Are you okay?" asked Aiden

Grace nodded trying to avoid her smile.

Aiden got up and put forward his hand to help her up.

She tumbled a little but Aiden supported her to stand upright.

"Thanks," she said as she tried balancing herself.

Aiden let go of her hand. "Why would you leave? You know the situation we are in. You were reckless, Grace. Who told you, you were torturing me?"

Grace looked down and coyly said,

"I am sorry. It was a spur. I was worried, seeing you like that."

Aiden raised his eyebrows, "You were worried about me?"

Grace looked right and left, then she stammered,

"Umm, er. Yeah. A…Alan! Can you find out who sent this?"

Alan smirked, "Sure."

Aiden held her hand again and said, "I am glad you are okay."

Grace smiled back.

Alan smirked and looked at Grace, "We will talk later!"

Grace nodded back, "We will."

Aiden spoke, "Let us go now."

Alan jumped to the driver's seat and Aiden sat next to him.

Grace hopped back.

Alan started the car and hummed mischievously.

There was silence.

Aiden was trying to wrap his brain around the fact that someone cared for him. He felt wonderful to feel important to someone again. Alan mischievously made jokes along the way, making Grace laugh every minute of the way. She felt better and distracted.

Tiny drops of water fell on her nose and lips as she rolled down the window and put her head out. She took a deep breath, enjoying every minute of this moment. She didn't want to let go.

This is how it feels to have best friends.
This is how it feels to have someone to rely on.

Her thoughts were interrupted by the car coming to a halt in front of the police station. Grace, Aiden and Alan walked inside the station and went to one of the police officers.

Alan looked around in surprise on finding Zoe.

"Hey Zoe. Long time. Is that really you?"

Zoe, turned back towards Alan. His smile widened and they hugged. Zoe was still the same.

"Woah, I last saw you in Vienna five years ago. You have gotten much more handsome. How is that even possible?" Zoe said.

Alan laughed and said, "Hey, you are the man in the uniform."

The duo chatted for a few minutes.

"Well, officer Zoe. I have a complaint to file."

Zoe instantly nodded his head and sat down in the chair.

"Ah, Grace. We meet again," he said looking at Grace.

Grace nodded her head reluctantly.

Alan spoke, "She was almost proven not innocent today."

Zoe nodded his head and continued scribbling something.

"It's good you're in charge of the investigation. One less reason for us to worry. We have so much to do before the next hearing."

Aiden interrupted, "Officer, I understand now that you were very occupied but I am disappointed. I was hoping for you to help me in the investigation and take some active charge of the detailing."

Zoe laughed uncomfortably and continued, "I understand you Mr. Aiden. I'm really sorry for my unavailability. Mr Noh didn't allow us to involve much. He and his lawyer took care of everything. Besides, he also hired a private detective.

Alan looked uncomfortably at Zoe.

He couldn't believe that this was the same guy who could fight the world for justice back in college and now is scared of Mr Noh.

Zoe continued, "What is the complaint?"

Alan slung forward his chair "Miss Grace was sent a dead mouse with a photo stained in red. It also contained a note which said that she must be hung to death for killing Zain and was signed off by a loyal fan of Zain."

Zoe nodded his head. "You know, after such controversial cases, it is possible for few toxic fans to lose their temper. It is punishable. I will try my best to issue a public statement. But punishing these teen fans severely may spoil the reputation of the police. Rest assured, we will try our best on finding the culprit."

Aiden stood up in slight dissatisfaction. He hesitantly said, "Thank you. I will look forward to hear from you, Officer."

Zoe smiled and helped them outside.

They got back into the car and sped away.

"I don't find this officer worthwhile. He hasn't helped at all."
Grace snugged, "He is pretty understanding. He even helped me
buy some time and contact a lawyer. Honestly, even I am
surprised that he didn't put efforts in the case. But that's obvious,
he has a family to feed. We know how ruthless Mr Noh can be."
"All right. Let's take you back home."
Grace stammered, "I… But..."
Aiden stopped her,"Don't worry *madame*. I am a gentleman and I
possess no axes. Alan will also stay with us until the murderer is
caught." Grace chuckled.
"Okay, I just need some more things from home."
Aiden nodded and hustled in the car.
They drove to Grace's apartment.

Chapter 7

Where is Aiden?

Grace switched on her flashlight and went inside her room. Aiden looked around her house. He finally had a minute to look around without an investigation on his mind. He noticed there were several certificates, trophies and appreciation awards on the shelves. Graduation certificates and photos hung on the wall. There was a small cupboard with a glass panel. It had few photo-frames. A little girl was sitting on a bench with her parents. He smiled. There were a few more photos of the young girl with her parents at different spots. Aiden chuckled looking at some of them. Grace looked adorable for sure.

Grace hurried out and said,

"I am sorry for hoarding your time."

Aiden smiled and helped her lock the gate.

"By the way, is your fever completely gone?"

Aiden smiled "Well, the medicine seemed to be magical."

Grace laughed, "Magical? It was a paracetamol."

Aiden touched his forehead, "Who said it was the pill?"

She blushed and looked away. Aiden smirked.

On the way back, Aiden looked outside the window. He saw the spot where Zain was murdered approach a few meters away.

A cold shudder replaced his thoughts.

Suddenly his glance hit a high-tech black car.

Wasn't this car here when we visited the shopkeeper?

He turned to Grace and asked,

"Was that black car there during the time of murder?"

Grace was surprised by the question.

She glanced outside and answered blankly,

"Yeah I guess. Um, yeah. It was there. Parked there in the same spot. I always looked at this car while passing by. It looks cool."

"Stop the car, Alan. Grace, go to my place. Take a cab. Call me when you reach and stay indoors. You'll be safe."

She questioned, but Aiden did not tell her anything further.

She placed her trust in Aiden and left.

Did he find something? A clue, perhaps?

Aiden rolled over the window and turned to Alan. He seemed to be explaining him something. It was inaudible from where Grace stood. Alan was dumbstruck. They seemed to have a serious conversation. *Maybe it is something personal,* she thought.

In the meantime, Grace waited by the store.

She saw Alan and Aiden speed away. A couple of people were gathered around her, talking, shopping, working and walking. She felt safe. She did not go back to her apartment. She did exactly what Aiden told her to do. She waited for a while, called a cab and went straight to Aiden's house.

She reached home and cooked herself a dinner. She waited for the boys to come, but when it got pretty late, she cleaned up and went to her room. She fell asleep.

The next morning, she woke up with heaviness.

She wanted to run away afar, but that would not help her prove her innocence. She looked outside if Aiden and Alan have come back home.

"Where were you?" Grace exclaimed looking at Alan.

He stretched and said, "Just some investigation. Get ready, Grace. We have an hour at most to appear in the courtroom."

Grace gasped, "Oh my God! Did I just oversleep?"

She rushed into her room to get ready.

Alan shook his head and let out a chuckle.

"Where is Aiden?" asked Grace at the breakfast table.

"He is busy, he'll see us in court," he poked the fork in the eggs.

"Oh my! He just got down from fever and look at him."

They finished breakfast and left the house.
The duo soon reached the court.

Grace took out a little box and said, "Alan, this is for you."
Alan widened his eyes, "What is this?"
Grace smiled, "Just a small farewell gift."
Alan smiled hesitantly.
He didn't know what to say.

Grace looked around, she whispered,
"Lawyer Stank is here. Where is Aiden? Why isn't he here yet."
"He'll be here any minute now. I'll call him."

Mr Noh walked to them. His lawyer Mr Stank followed.
He looked at their desperate faces and commented,
"Oh my! Has that lawyer run away?"
Alan flinched. He was furious.
The lawyer smiled coyly.
Grace's mind was all over the place.
She knew, Aiden wouldn't desert them at the last moment.
Is he okay? Did he faint again? What if the murderer confronted him? Did he get involved in an accident?
She shook her thoughts away and walked in anyway.
It was time.

Alan tried to reassure her.
"Everything will be okay."
But would it?

Chapter 8

Everything's Okay Grace

The judge arrived. She was nervous and scared.

The room greeted him and the court resumed.

The judge looked around. "Where is your lawyer?"

"He will be here any minute now," said Alan.

The judge looked at him in disbelief.

He rolled his eyes and continued, "I will proceed with my judgement as Mr Aiden has failed to appear before the jury."

Just as the Judge was about to continue, he saw Aiden at the court room entrance. He hurried inside and spoke, breathing heavily.

"Your honour. I am sorry for the delay." Everyone looked at him.

"I have a physical evidence. Please, may I present it to the court.

The judge shook his head and said, "Okay, continue."

Lawyer Stank was about to get up to object when the Judge eyed him to sit down. Aiden looked at Grace who was looking at him with questioning eyes. He smiled.

"Mr Stank, I think you said that the reason my client is a murderer is that there is no physical evidence, right? I have it right here. I seek permission, Your Honor, to play this video."

The judge nodded. Everyone turned to the projector.

Aiden hit play and the video started with a glitch. The screen showed Grace, walking out of the shop followed by Zain. The video quality was low but out of the thin mist, they were visible. Suddenly, as soon as the sunset, there was a blackout. Things were still visible as the camera had night vision. Soon, a man in black jeans and a black t-shirt with a knife in his hand was spotted. He was tall and muscular, exactly how Grace described.

He pounced at Zain and whispered something in his ears.

Zain wriggled to be set free but the man stabbed him deeply.

Grace turned back and rushed to him. But the murderer cleverly pushed the body towards Grace as she held it in her arms. Suddenly the street lights returned. Therefore he ran away at utmost speed, leaving the blood-stained Zain with Grace.

Grace stood up and looked at the screen with drops of tears falling down her cheeks. The most hideous incident in her life was displayed on the screen, she wept silently. Mr Noh got up slowly and fell on his knees, he shivered up to the screen and touched the screen and whimpered. The courtroom was drop-dead silent except for the weep of Mr Noh.

The judge took a deep sigh, he continued,

"Weren't all the CCTVs out of order. How did you find this?"

Aiden smiled, "Your Honour, CCTVs were out of order. But in our stained destiny, a ray of hope glimmered through a car. One of the cars parked in the area had a DashCam turned on all the while along. Yesterday, I noticed the car parked at the same place again. It was a new car, so it definitely had a camera. I found out the owner after some research and he obliged to help in any way needed. As you can see, it recorded the incident clearly. After a lot of searching through different time arrangements, I found it just an hour before the court could proceed."

The judge made some notes and announced,
"Keeping in point all the evidences, I announce Miss Grace not guilty and request the prosecution to take necessary steps to catch the murderer. The local cops are advised to start an investigation immediately. The court is adjourned."

The judge got up and left.

There were shocked murmurings in the audience as people dispersed slowly. Mr. Noh looked at Grace with eyes filled with guilt, but Grace had her eyes fixed on Aiden. The people in the room started dispersing and there was a calm silence.

Mr. Hudson had a sense of proudness on his face. Grace took a step towards Aiden. Her eyes were filled with gratitude. She hugged him right in the court. Aiden was surprised by her gesture, but he hugged her back, caressing her hair.
"Everything's okay, Grace."
Grace wrapped her hand around his back and Aiden took a breath of relief. He let out a tear filled with happiness, "We did it."
"What would I do without you guys?" Grace whispered.

Alan was sitting on the sofa fidgeting with his laptop when Aiden entered the house. Aiden switched on the television and flipped to the news channel. Grace came outside her room with blue pyjamas and light blue tee with semi wet hair. She sat down along with the two, fixing her eyes on the television set.

One of the most popular idols, Zain Noh was murdered a few days ago and the prime accused, was released not guilty today. The murderer is suspected to be a young man who wore a black jacket and black mask. The video of Zain being murdered has surfaced on the social media, shaking the virtual world."

"How did the video go viral?" asked Aiden.
Grace followed, "Isn't that confidential information?"

"Well, I did it." Alan spoke, still hitting the keys of the laptop.
Aiden looked at Alan with furrowed eyebrows.
Grace turned to him open-mouthed.

"What? Why are you staring at me?"
"Why did you do that?" Aiden asked.
He rolled his eyes, "This is the virtual world. I posted the video with an anonymous username and it hit the clouds. This is a live proof Aiden. People are finally believing it and standing up for Grace. People are trying to identify him and the comments are filled with apologies for Grace. This way, the toxic comments are reduced and the fans will understand she is not guilty.
"Hmm. Okay. Good job." Aiden said keeping a straight face.
Grace nearly screamed, "You're the best. Thank you, Alan."

"Let's celebrate and have a terrace party!" Alan screamed.
Grace squealed, "with a movie, wine and lots of food."
Aiden smirked, trying to hide his excitement,
"Well, whatever. I will get the projector from the store room."
Grace and Alan began prepping for the party.

In the evening, they went on the terrace. The decor was perfect. Grace picked out some wine. The trio sat on the floor and played a horror movie. It was the first time for Grace to have fun with friends. On the terrace, Aiden poured 2 glasses of wine, one for himself and Grace. They went to the corner of the roof, watching the stars. Alan decided to leave them alone for a while and hoarded the snacks.

Grace sipped the wine, closed her eyes and whispered,
"The weather and the view is pretty today."
Aiden looked at Grace, her brown hair flowing freely in the air, a soft smile adoring her face, her pink lips curved in gloss, Aiden replied, "Definitely, very pretty."

He pulled her hands closer.

Her face was just a few centimetres away from his.

Grace gulped softly as she looked down at the rosy lips of Aiden and his warm hands not letting go.

"Don't leave me alone again, Grace. You are very important to me. I..." his voice trailed.

Grace blushed. "I am? Who am I to you?"

Aiden looked away and smiled.

"You owe me, remember? I'll call in my chit."

"Happy New Life." his soft lips came closer as they touched the cheeks of Grace.

He got up and walked away. "You…!" She growled.

That night, Grace twirled and turned in her bed,

What was the meaning of that kiss?

Was it just a friendly greeting or does he have feelings for me?

Grace banged her face on her pillow.

Soon she woke up to the small chirping of the birds. She took a shower and went out to see Aiden had already cooked today. She smiled and sat at the table. "Morning Grace!"

"Good morning!" Grace sat down and placed a cheese toast on her plate and said, "Guys! I have something to say."

Aiden put down his newspaper and replied, "Go ahead!"

"Well, I am thinking of starting work again and I will go searching for a law firm from today."

"How about we all three start something together?" said Aiden.

Alan and Grace instantly smiled at the idea.

Two Days Later

It was a beautiful Thursday morning. Aiden had a tiny flat in Camber's street that he previously used as his office. Alan, and Grace had already started with the paperwork. Grace bought a template that read *AGA Firms - Let Justice Prevail.*

The trio stood in front of the office proudly, the golden template glittered in the sunlight. The trio walked inside the office together. There were three different cabins - small but detailed. They had a computer, desk and few other accessories. Grace hopped in the middle cabin and Alan and Aiden took one side each. They decorated their cabins respectively and celebrated the opening with a bottle of champagne.

Alan got busy with a few legal matters whereas Grace got busy with the paperwork. Aiden informed his legal co-mates about his new firm and worked on advertising and marketing.

The sheer silence was broken by a sudden ring of the phone.

Alan picked up, he nodded for a while before he picked up his coat and said "On duty. Let's go."
Aiden shrieked, "Why? What happened?"
"We may be a step closer to the murderer." Alan replied.

The trio rushed down the street to reach the police station. Officer Zoe was waiting for them outside his cabin, and as soon as they arrived, he called them inside. He said, "I was working on the harassment case of Grace and I think we have a trace here."
Aiden jumped, "What trace?"
The officer explained, "Well, here check the CCTV footage. Luckily, the criminal was intelligent enough to erase the footage of the building, but he forgot the aisle! Look, a man in black clothes walked outside the aisle nearly at that time. He is covering his face and avoiding the cameras."
Alan interrupted and said,
"He has the same physique as the murderer."
Zoe hit on the desk and exclaimed, "Exactly."
Aiden shook his head, "Something is still missing."
Zoe instantly asked, "But what?"
Aiden gasped, "When he deleted every footage on the streets, it would be foolish of him to leave the one on the aisle. He isn't foolish. He is damn clever. Maybe he wants us to notice him."
Alan nodded, "Now, that you mention, it is strange."
"Alan, let's go and check the streets. We may find something."

Zoe nodded, "I would have come with you, but I am stuck with this terrace murder near Grace's house."
Aiden got up with Alan and they started to leave.
Grace said, "Aiden, you go ahead. I have somewhere to go."
Aiden tried to stop her but Grace said,
"Don't worry, go ahead. This is important to me."
Aiden nodded and left with Alan.

Grace went back to the police station.
She met Zoe. "So?" he asked.
Grace looked straight in his eyes and said,
"Which doctor is in charge of the terrace murder case?"
"I cannot reveal it to you. Until you are in charge of the case."

Grace nodded with a sigh and walked out. I don't know but my sixth sense says that the man in the tank was somewhat familiar. *I need to go to the very bottom of this.*

While walking out, she dashed into a man.
The man was decked in wrinkles and his eyes were swollen as if he was crying a lot.
Grace instantly apologised, "Oh my! I am sorry, sir."
The old man tumbled and lifted his tiny head towards Grace.
His little red eyes squinted, whispering, "Grace?"
Grace looked up. "How do you know me, sir?"
"We met at the street last year," he coughed and said,
"I am the owner of that deserted building."

Grace's mind raced back a year ago.
This same old man was carrying a lot of luggage. He had just moved in. Grace helped him safely place it in his cab. He had introduced himself as the owner of that building who was going

to be transferred to Melbourne, Australia.

"Yes. I remember. It's been long. Are you back here now?"

The old man burst into tears, "Due to the murder and the incident on the terrace, I am brought here as a suspect. But I have no money to hire a lawyer, dear. I'm lost right now."

Grace smiled and said, "I will take your case, sir. Any nominal fees, I will accept it. You need not worry at all."

The old man wiped his tears, "You will help me? Really?"

Grace nodded, "I will." She handed him her card.

"Thank you so much, I'll come see you soon."

She rushed back to the cabin.

"Mr. Zoe? Let me re-introduce myself," she cleared her throat.

"I am the lawyer of the defendant in the terrace case."

Zoe looked up and let out a gasp.

"You are quick. Anyways, the doctor is Dr. Knuckles."

Chapter 9

Everything's Coming Up, Grace

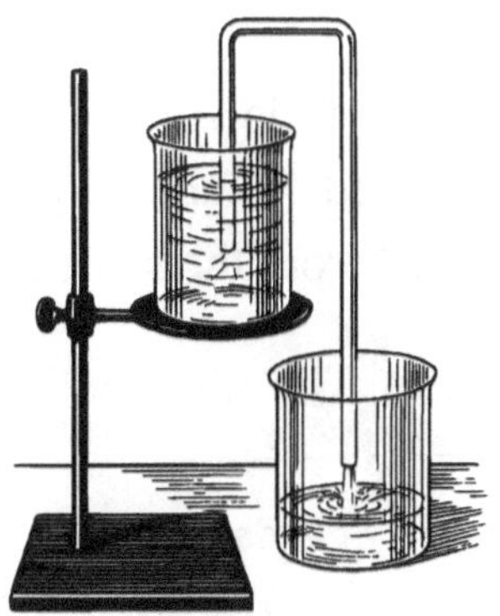

Grace reached the lab and went to the doctor in charge. Grace saw a man, probably in his forties, wearing a white coat with grey hair, closely looking through some files.

Grace knocked on the door, "Doctor Knuckles?"

"Yes? How may I help you?" he looked up at her.

"I am Grace, the lawyer for Mr. Stews for the terrace murder case. I needed some information about the same,"

She handed him her card, "Can you tell me about the victim?"

"Alright, this way, Ms. Grace." Grace followed him in.

"Here is the body. This is Mr Auray."

He was a photographer and nearly 24 years old."
Grace kept staring at his face, "Why is his name so similar?"
"He was a famous guy. He won awards and organised many elite exclusive exhibitions in the city."
Grace shook her head, "How was he killed?"
The doctor sighed, "He was stabbed to death and left in the tank."
"Stabbed? This is so sad. He was so young." Grace murmured.
"And a good person too. He graduated from the University of St. Maria in New York."
Grace's eyes widened, "St. Maria? In New York?"
The doctor nodded and asked "Yeah, Why?"
"Well, Zain also graduated from the same University."

On the other side, Alan and Aiden were looking for clues.
Aiden murmured, "Nothing yet, probably it was a wrong hunch."
Alan shook his head, "I don't think so. Let's keep going."
Alan, "Right. Why don't we search the box he gave to Grace?"
Aiden looked at him, "Ah. Yes! Where is the box?"
Alan stammered, "Uh oh, um - I actually I threw it."
"What? Where?"
"The window outside the hallway."

Aiden rolled his eyes, "Let's go there."

The duo went to the area facing the window. It was a small road surrounded by grass. After half an hour of rummaging, they found the box buried in one of the bushes. It was still stinking. He threw all the contents of the box down. A photo and then a small paper fell down.

I knew you'd come here. I am impressed that you're smarter than I thought. But now you'd better stop looking for me. I don't give a third warning. Let me finish my mission and you won't be hurt.

Aiden read the note again, "Mission? What mission?"

Alan spoke, "More murders?"

"Let's go home and discuss this with Grace," Aiden said.

Grace was already home. She had rummaged through the drawers and pulled out the older case files. She went through the contents and spoke out loud to nobody in particular, "I was right."

"What is it?" asked Aiden who was watching her from the door. Alan stood right behind him.

"Sit down. We need to talk," she said waving the files at him.

So, you mean that Zain and Auray both were best friends at the university? And both were stabbed to death?" Alan spoke.

Grace nodded, "Yes. I knew I had seen him somewhere. At my old office, I saw him a few times with Zain. Auray was one out of the four who nearly killed a 17-year-old boy in a fight."

"What? An assault?" asked Alan. He did not know this.

"Yes. It was very brutal. The boy is still in a coma and is critical. I had all proof against Zain, but Mr Noh never let me continue."

"There is so much bad in the world, Grace and there is only so much that we can do. But what matters is if we try. And you did." Aiden said, looking at her with empathy in his eyes.

"So," Alan spoke, "Zain was murdered on a Friday. Auray was murdered the previous Friday. Tomorrow is a Friday."
"If this is related to the assault case then there is a possibility another murder will happen tomorrow night."
"But who? and why?" Grace tried to connect the dots.
But there weren't *enough* dots to connect.

Aiden explained his theory.
"There were four people involved. Out of them, two were killed. So the third and fourth are definitely in danger. Grace, Alan, we need to find these two."
"The other two scumbags - er, sorry - I mean guys are, Baryon and Kian. Baryon is a rich heir of a soap and cosmetic company. He is now in Venice, whereas Kian lives here, in this city by the border. As far as I know, he lives alone with his fiancée."

Alan asked, "How do you know all this?"
"How can I ever forget a failed case?"

Alan nodded, "I agree, we cannot let him get away this time."
"But we should be careful. He has already killed two people in cold blood. We cannot afford to make any mistakes."
"Let's first meet Kian tomorrow morning. We need to alert him."
"He needs to know now. We'll reach there only by the evening."
"No officers involved. This is on us." Aiden replied.

That night neither of the three slept. They knew that if the guess is right, a man's life was at risk. It was up to them to save him.

The next morning, all three of them looked pale. Alan and Grace hardly ate. Aiden ate well. He looked at both of them,
"Chill. Everything will be fine"
Alan looked at his side, "Everything is coming up, Grace."

Grace dialled Kian as soon as she finished eating from her phone. Someone picked up.

"Hey Kian, I am Grace."
A low and scared voice replied,
"That lawyer? Why are you calling me?"
"I heard both your partners were killed."
Kian was going to break down.
"I saw the news. Please save me. Please."

Grace handed over the phone to Aiden.
"We'll help you. You just need to follow instructions carefully."
Kian stammered, "I will, I just don't want to die."
"He will probably show up in the late evening. My team will come there today. Just don't inform the police. It will alert him."

Kian nodded and said, "Okay. I will not inform anybody."
"Don't go out anywhere alone for now. Stay home."

Aiden called Baryon. He told him to return back to the city or law will get to him. To protect his company's reputation, he decided to reach the city by the evening.

That afternoon was the slowest afternoon of their lives. They tried to keep busy with notes, research and making murder boards. When it was nearly late afternoon, the trio left to see Kian. They reached the end of the city in an hour. Kian's house was huge. The murderer would have a lot of ways to break in if it wasn't protected.

The team took their positions in hiding.
Grace called Kian, "We are here. You're safe but you need to continue your usual routine. If the murderer makes a move on you, we'll take over."
Kian whimpered, "I am screwed. Why is he after me?"
Aiden snatched the phone, "After saving you from the killer, I will teach you a good lesson. How could you be so irresponsible? You nearly killed a boy. Now shut it."
Kian whimpered, "I already get nightmares about that boy, I am so sorry. I was so immature."
Aiden cut the phone.
Hours ticked like a ticking bomb.
The sun set soon. It was dark now.

Alan spoke, "It is over 3 hours dude. I guess we were wrong."
Aiden pounced on Alan, "Shhh...Shut up!"
"Look! I guess that's him," Alan pointed towards a tall man.
Grace took a step back, holding Aiden's hands. The black figure moved closer to the house in a few minutes. He was just a few paces from the grass where the trio was. Grace was the closest to him. He had a mask on but she could see the scar on his neck. *Yes, That's him. This is the same guy that stabbed Zain*, she thought. Grace looked at Alan and Aiden and nodded, indicating that she recognizes him.

Aiden, Grace and Alan sat there without moving. The man moved towards the window instead of the door. He hitched it open and entered inside. The window slammed shut behind him.
Aiden got up, "He looks more dangerous than I thought. I will go inside first. Alan, you call the cops. We'll catch him red-handed. I will hold him for 15 minutes.

"No way! This can't be your plan. He has a knife," said Grace
Aiden smiled, "Don't worry. I will take care of it."
Alan rushed to the street shivering and dialled 911.
Aiden unlocked the window and sneaked inside.
Grace stood outside, whispering a prayer. *Please keep him safe.*

Aiden reached inside and crawled to the living room. He saw the man holding Kian by his collar as he screamed,
"You will repay for all you have done. I want to hear you beg, and whimper. I want to see you scared and hopeless."
The man in the mask raised his knife to stab Kian
Kian closed his eyes in fear.

Meanwhile, Grace got restless. She began to play a hundred different scenarios in her head about how this could end. She hated the places her brain was taking her.
Alan ran to her, "They're on their way. I hope Aiden is safe."
"I really hope he is. Should we go in?" said Grace.
"Let's trust him, Grace."

Back at the house, drops of blood fell on the ground. The dark red blood created big spots on the furnished carpet. Kian opened his eyes filled with tears. He looked at his body, he wasn't hurt. When he looked up, he saw blood oozing from Aiden's body. At this sight, he fell back on the floor, unconscious.

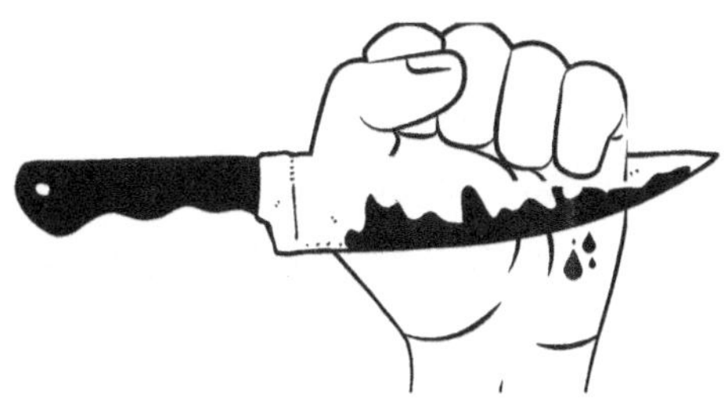

The murderer's eyes widened. His eyes turned red in rage.
"I warned you. I told you not to interfere."
Aiden shouted back, still holding the knife,
"I can't let you kill more people. Who are you?"
The murderer laughed and turned furious, "
"You didn't identify me yet?"

Aiden threw the knife away and attacked the man. A straight blow on his cheeks and the man fell on the sofa. They both got into a heavy fistfight. Aiden tried to hold him down but he was strong. A loud scream filled the room. Aiden gasped in frustration and attacked the man again but he flung Aiden to the other side of the room, smashing him into the glass table. He took his chance and grabbed the fallen knife.

Outside, Grace and Alan couldn't hold back anymore. The noises coming from the house terrified them. They had to go in. They could no longer wait for the police. They entered the house. Grace and Alan froze at the sight. Their jaws dropped as they saw the man standing over Aiden raising the knife to stab him.
"You were a good man. I had no intention of killing you. But you tried protecting the wrong person. Bye-bye Aiden."

A loud shrill echoed in the room.
Aiden screamed as the murderer dropped his knife,
Grace had jumped in front of Aiden. She was hurt.
"Why did you…?" his voice trailed off.
Aiden fell on the floor crying, his eyes widened in shock.
What just happened? His body was numb.
Grace's shirt was covered in red.

The murderer was taken aback. He turned to run when a police officer put a gun on his forehead, "Dare to move?"
Alan stepped forward, "The ambulance is on its way here."
"Why did you stab her?" Aiden said and threw a punch.
He was about to throw another before the cops held him back.
The murderer shouted, "I didn't kill her, She jumped into the fire. I just wanted to hurt you a little, enough to finish my mission."
"Who are you?" Aiden asked and pulls off his mask.
"Hey! Now, you recognise me?"
Aiden was shocked! "You?"
"Yep. I thought I would silently finish my task but you three are so nosy..." The cops handcuffed him.
Alan growled, "How could you? I thought you were a friend."

Chapter 10

Destiny Stained, Again?

"Friend? I hate this word. I hated the fact that you are involved in this. I hate the fact that this girl is lying half dead on the floor and I also hate the fact I couldn't kill Kian."

Aiden was frustrated. He clenched his fists and said, "Zoe! Enough! Officers, please take him away before I strangle him."

The officers dragged the handcuffed Zoe to the jeep.

Alan sprinkled water on Kian's face and gave him a glass of water. Kian woke up to the sight of Grace being taken away in a stretcher, bleeding. Aiden followed Grace with teary eyes into the ambulance. "Stay with me, Grace," he whispered all the way.

Grace was rushed to the ICU. The doctors said that the wound was not so deep and they had brought her in time but she had to undergo surgery immediately. Alan followed the ambulance and arrived at the hospital along with Kian. He helped Aiden with the paperwork and paid the bill.

All they had to do now, was wait.

Meanwhile, a nurse came to him and said, "She'll be fine. You're bleeding yourself. Please, come this way. You will need first aid. Did you get into a fight?" Aiden nodded and followed her in.

In a few minutes, the nurse and Aiden came out.
Aiden had bandages all over his neck, arms and face.

"How is she?" he asked.
"How are you?" Alan raised his eyebrows.
"I'm very much alive. Now tell me, how is she?"
"She is fine. The surgery was successful. She's in observation."

Aiden sighed in relief, "I think I'm in love with her."
Alan smiled, "I know."

A few hours later, Grace was shifted to the observation room.
"She's a fighter," Alan whispered as they entered.
"She sure is," Aiden said and held her hands in his.

It was morning already.
The sunlight crept into the room through the window.

The doctor entered the room to conduct a check-up.
"She can be discharged tomorrow," he smiled. "You're a strong lady, Miss Grace." He handed a prescription to Aiden and left.
Aiden turned towards Grace, caressed her hair and said,
"This is what I love the most about you. You could fight with the world and win, your confidence and..." he looked into her eyes.
"and how beautiful you look even on a hospital bed."
"I like you, Grace. I really do." Aiden blushed for the first time.
"I like you more, Aiden," she whispered.
There was silence for a while.

Alan came with breakfast and stood at the door.

He cleared his throat, "May I come in?"

"Hey Alan," said Grace, "...thanks for everything."

"You look good!" Alan hugged her tight.

Aiden shot a glare at him and they all burst in laughter.

"So he's your boyfriend now, eh." Alan said.

They smiled at each other and nodded.

It was a long night, but the morning started with a smile.

"Kian was asked to come to the station for a statement so I've dropped him there. One of us will have to go down there later today," Alan said. "So, I'll go. You stay with her, Aiden."

The Next Day

Grace was discharged. Aiden took her home.

Alan joined them after. Grace felt a lot better already.

She insisted on joining them at the station in the evening.

"I want to see that man go to jail. Let's finish what we started."

"Only if you let me carry you to the station," joked Aiden.

That evening, Alan, Aiden and Grace went to the police station.

Zoe was held in the station jail, waiting to be interrogated.

They walked to Zoe. Aiden was curious to know why he did what he did and what he meant by completing his mission.

Aiden asked, "How are you related to the abuse case?"

Zoe rest his head on the chair, closed his eyes and said,

"Doesn't it hurt, Aiden? Losing a close one? Those people you were trying to save tried to kill my only brother. They took away my only happiness from me. My brother is still in the hospital struggling between life and death. What did the law do? Let the criminals go? I was a good officer, but I couldn't see my brother suffer everyday while these unjust criminals roamed outside, enjoying every bit of life. I was helpless. This was the last straw. I don't care about the consequences. I just had one mission. Erase their happiness and surrender to the law."

"I understand what you must've gone through. After my best friend killed himself, I also wanted to finish those idiots. But I chose to do it the right way. They're behind bars now. Your mistake was that you chose the wrong way," said Aiden.

Later at Zoe's hearing, Kian accepted his crime and confessed his wrong-doings. Kian and Baryon were behind the bars for assault. Zoe was imprisoned for life.

Six Months Later

AGA Firms became one of the most successful law firms in the city. Aiden, Grace and Alan also took up a lot of pro-bono cases whenever they could. Their hard work, dedication and efforts had paid off. Today, they completed their 50th win together.

Grace was getting ready for their celebration when she suddenly received a text, "Grace. Emergency! Terrace. Now!"
She froze. *What happened?* She rushed upstairs.

The terrace was pitch black.
In a few seconds, the lights turned on.
Grace looked around in awe. The place was decorated. Aiden stood in the centre with a black suit, red roses and a ring in his hand. He came forward and bent on his knees.
Grace gasped. "Aiden?"
Aiden slipped on the glistening diamond on her hand, "Forever?"
Grace hugged him with teary eyes, "Forever!"
The sky lit in fireworks. Alan, Mr. Hudson and her mother followed with little heart balloons cheering for them. It began to snow. Aiden and Grace looked at each other and smiled.

Grace thought, *Each story has darkness, but without it we would never spot the star made for us. We fall and we learn. We fight and we love, In this destiny, my star came wrapped in a suit and a heavy attitude, but he made me love me. The right person painted my stained destiny with the colors of love!*

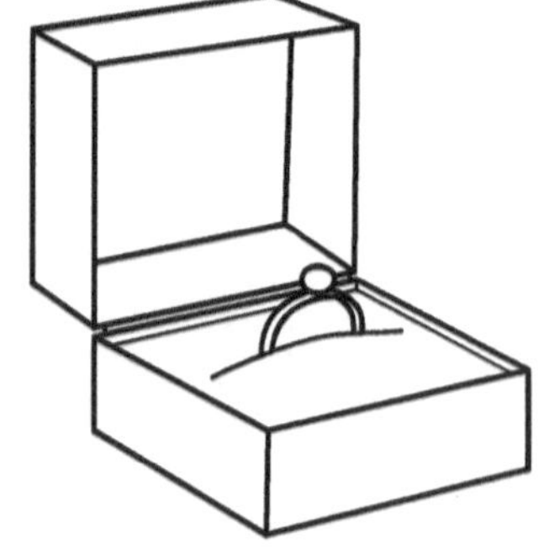

About the Author

Shradha Agarwal is a 16 year old girl from Siva Sivani Public School, Visakhapatnam, Andhra Pradesh, India.

She started her journey of writing very young. By the time she turned 13, she had already written poems and short stories. Shradha enjoys binging on Kdrama and listening to music. Her favourite band is Kpop. Shradha also is an avid reader. Her favourite genres include rom-com, mystery and fiction. She journals occasionally and tries her hand at various other hobbies.

More of a free soul, she likes speaking on various issues and topics and also aspires to become a public speaker. She describes herself as a wanderlust. She believes travelling is one of the most essential spheres of her life.

You can find her on Instagram by the username @shradha_ag_5

Acknowledgements

Stories By Children is a dream project for me that was inspired by my nephew who wrote a beautiful story and it went unnoticed, lying in the corner of a room, incomplete and unheard. It is a pleasure to see these young budding writers grow, learn and showcase their talent to the world. We are all but just a medium through which they can take their words to the readers. But the dedication, energy, time and skill that goes into the making of each and every piece of work - a poem or a story - is remarkable. Every writer is important to us and so is every piece of work.

Thanks to all the children who have participated in the Novel Writing Contest 2021 and made it a successful one. We hope to see the same, or perhaps more, enthusiasm and love from you all next year. Special thanks to the parents who have encouraged their children to pursue their love for writing and helped them explore their skills. Your support means a lot.

Thanks to our sponsors - Bangaloreblaze Girls' High School Bangalore, St. Antony's Public School Hubli, Sanskaar English Medium School Hubli for volunteering and contributing to help us keep this platform free for all. Thanks to **Inkfeathers Publishing** for helping us take this book worldwide. Special mentions to Uma Bokil guiding us through the publishing process. Thanks to Kashish Lewis and her team for designing and editing the book.

Last but not the least, thanks to every person who has purchased this book. You have contributed and supported our community and the author in your own little way.

About the Judge

Manoj Vaz is an award-winning copywriter with 3 decades of experience handling over 50 blue - chip clients. Born in the middle-class underbelly of Mumbai, he started his advertising career as a copywriter in Sam Balsara's Madison Advertising.

Later, he realised that he was too independent to toe the line and started his own creative boutique - Touché Communications in 1991. 25 years later, he realised that writing for clients did not give him the creative satisfaction he craved. It dawned upon him that being in a hectic, deadline ridden industry will never give him the time to follow his own dream. He shut down his running ad agency the day he turned 50 and started writing.

His first book, Tinsel was published in 2015 and soon climbed up the bestseller charts. He wrote more books like Kidnapping, Meth Mystery, Random Musings. His recent book is titled Queendom, published by **Inkfeathers Publishing.**

Manoj Vaz's Books

Queendom - In the year 1178-79, a young Sultan Mu'izz ad-Din Muhammad Ghori of Ghor (Afghanistan) gathered a large force and marched towards Anhilwara, the capital of Gujarat. This was to be his gateway to India. But he had to contend with a Rajput warrior queen. In the history of Chalukya Rajputs of India lies buried the true story of a valiant mother-daughter duo - Kuram Devi and her mother Naiki Devi. Queendom tells the remarkable story of arguably the oldest examples of empowered women in the world. Get the book on Amazon or the Inkfeathers Bookstore.

The Magic Chest - This series is a pack of mystery and crime solving stories for teens but can be enjoyed by all ages as well. The first book of the series, ***The Kidnapping*** is the story of a gang of kinds who are naughty, playful, intelligent, internet savvy and adventurous. The group is led by Mannu who is a brave 14 year old boy. The cases they solve are also crimes that happen every day in a city like Mumbai. Tackling contemporary crimes, the series also aims to install values like courage, loyalty, friendship and teamwork among children.

Our Sponsors

Bangaloreblaze Girls' High School

Teachers Colony, 1st Stage, Nagarabhavi, Bangalore, Karnataka

Sanksaar English Medium School

Sanskaar Nagar, Kusugal Road, Keshwapur, Hubli, Karnataka

In 2007, the Hubli Education Society laid the foundation for an ideal school, focused on the wholesome and overall development of the learners, in the spheres of cognitive, kinesthetic, social and moral development. Thus Sanskaar English Medium School was born as a living and transformational force. All the 11 Batches of the grade 10 students cleared the board exams with 100 % results. Our students won Interschool General Championship, 3 times in a single year, just before the COVID-19 stalled our efforts briefly. During the pandemic, Sanskaar conducted online classes effectively with the help of a customized mobile app.

Each classroom is enabled with an internet connection and digital smart boards. All the classrooms in Bal-Sanskaar (Kindergarten) have digital boards, a separate dining hall, an assembly, a play area and attached toilets.

With the school motto, "Vidya Vinayena Shobhate" which means, *Knowledge is graceful because of humility* the school strives to imbibe knowledge.

St. Antony's Public School

St. Antony School Bus Stop, Vidya Nagar, Hubli, Karnataka

Our education society is located in Siddeshwar Park, Vidyanagar, Hubli. Our education society lays claims to have a sound foundation in the holistic approach to the development of individual students. The school has been striving to offer an effective child-centric education that concentrates on the all-around development of the body, mind and spirit.

Students of today face a world that continually demands to equip them with current knowledge and abilities; it demands them to be life-long learners in an ever-changing scenario.

As everyone knows, a tree has to start its life from seed and if it is nurtured carefully, it would emerge into a big tree, similarly, we started in a very small way and now we have crossed many years of struggle to achieve the goals of excellence. Knowledge is a tool that helps everyone to dig deep into the reserves, make a person confident and raise their self-esteem. We impart self-respect, honesty, hard work, dedication, sincerity which are the five elements to yield the best results in life.

Inkfeathers Publishing

India's most author friendly publishing platform

A content-driven bootstrapped startup, which has now become India's most author-friendly platform, helping young aspiring writers to publish & sell their books globally, supporting them in building their network for good outreach and connecting them with the media & entertainment industry so that their write-ups can transform into motion content. We stand with our writers' hand in hand throughout their journey. Inkfeathers is connected to thousands of writers & artists globally, who believe in the magic of telling stories. This stream of connectivity with the writers, the fact that everyone has a unique detail or edge to their story makes Inkfeathers proud to partner with these young literary as well as collaborative minds.

If you are looking for a book publisher who understands your needs and vision for a book, Inkfeathers Publishing is the only publishing platform you need. Publish your book and let us take it to the audience it deserves globally.

Book a free publishing consultation with Inkfeathers today.
Call **+91 8055931667** or email at **publish@inkfeathers.com**

Theme Writing Contest

Every alternate month a Theme Writing contest is conducted where every age group is allotted a particular topic to write about. Theme Writing Contests are held for both story-tellers and poets who wish to submit their work for free on the given topic. Every odd Theme Writing Contest is for stories and every even Theme Writing Contest is for poetry. Winners receive medals and prizes.
Theme Writing 1, 3, 5 and so on - Story Writing Contest
Theme Writing 2, 4, 6 and so on - Poetry Writing Contest

Most Popular Story/Poetry Contest

After every Theme Writing Contest, a Most Popular Story/Poetry Contest is conducted. This happens every alternate month and starts as soon as the Theme Writing Contest is concluded. In this contest, the participants of the Theme Writing Contest need to share and popularize their work with the help of friends and family. The participants with the most bells/likes or comments win a medal and a free book. Each bell and comment carry points. The participant with the most points will be awarded.

Reading Challenge

After every Theme Writing Contest, a Reading Challenge quiz is conducted. This happens every alternate month and starts as soon as the Theme Writing Contest is concluded. In this contest, readers must read all the selected stories of the TWC contest in their age group and answer a quiz of 10 questions from the stories to win. The participant with the highest score is awarded a medal and a free book. Anyone can take part in this contest. Regular readers who are above 18 can participate in the 15+ category.

Novel Writing / Mega Story Writing Contest

This event only happens annually. Writers are encouraged to write novels in the age group of 11-18 and mega stories in the 7-10 years age group. The Registrations shall be open starting from February every year and submission will close in the month of August. Winners List will be declared every year on the 25th of November - that marks the anniversary of Stories By Children. The winners of this contest will be published in print and featured on our website every year. Winners of this contest also receive trophies, certificates and more.

INKFEATHERS PUBLISHING

India's Most Author Friendly Publishing House

Stay updated about the latest anthologies, events,
exclusive offers, contests, product giveaways
and other things that we do to support authors.

Inkfeathers Publishing

@InkfeathersPublishing

@_Inkfeathers

@Inkfeathers

Inkfeathers.com

We'd love to connect with you!